A SECRET WISH

A SECRET WISH
Published by Barbara Freethy
First Printing: January 2012
ISBN: 978-0-9836517-9-6

This is a work of fiction. Names, characters, places, and incidents are products of the author's imagination or are used fictitiously. Any resemblance to actual events, locales, organizations or persons, living or dead, is entirely coincidental.

For information contact:
Barbara Freethy
barbara@barbarafreethy.com

Publishing Services by KLFpub.com

PRAISE FOR THE NOVELS OF BARBARA FREETHY

"Freethy has a gift for creating complex, appealing characters and emotionally involving, often suspenseful, sometimes magical stories." -- Library Journal

"Barbara Freethy delivers strong and compelling prose." – Publishers Weekly

"Fans of Nora Roberts will find a similar tone here, framed in Freethy's own spare, elegant style." – Contra Costa Times

"A fresh and exciting voice in women's romantic fiction." – Susan Elizabeth Phillips

"Freethy skillfully keeps readers on the hook." – Booklist

"Superlative." – Debbie Macomber

"If there is one author who knows how to deliver vivid stories that tug on your emotions, it's Barbara Freethy." – Romantic Times

Also available from Barbara Freethy

In The WISH SERIES

Just A Wish Away (#2)

Complete booklist available at
www.barbarafreethy.com

Chapter One

Liz Kelly stepped up to the waist-high ledge that ran around the tenth-floor roof of St. John's Hospital. Although the roof was a popular retreat for doctors and nurses on break, it was quiet on this Friday night. Just past seven o'clock, anyone not on duty had already left the building, trying to get one last warm and sunny weekend in before fall turned into winter. She loved the view from the roof, especially as night settled over the city. From her vantage point, she could see the cable cars chugging up and down the steep hills of San Francisco, the colorful sails on the boats in the Marina, and the lights of the Golden Gate Bridge blazing through a bank of fog hovering over the ocean.

The view always inspired her. Up here she felt like she could be anyone and do anything. Unfortunately, she couldn't seem to turn the inspiration into action. As soon as she went back inside, she returned to her old ways, to her safe, risk-free existence that was getting her nowhere. She liked being a nurse, but the rest of her life was in shambles. She'd lived with a half dozen roommates in the last decade, changed apartments three times, and had just been dumped by her boyfriend of three years.

What annoyed her most was that Kyle had broken up with her. She should have been the one to break up with him. He'd fallen far short of her expectations, but she'd never been able to pull the trigger on their relationship. She'd always been afraid of being thirty and alone. Well, that's exactly what had happened. But tonight was the start of a new decade. She needed to get it together, take a risk, and stop being paralyzed by fear of making the wrong decision. She had to take charge of her life and stop letting her future be defined by her past. She needed to do something...

What that *something* was, she wasn't quite sure, but she intended to find out.

Mental pep talk over, she opened a small bakery box from Faith's Fancies and slid out a miniature gourmet cupcake dotted with pink icing and chocolate stars. Chocolate was her passion, especially rich, dark chocolate. Taking a pink candle out of her purse, she stuck it in the icing, and raised the cake to the starlit sky. "Happy birthday to me."

Her muttered words seemed to mock her newfound resolve, so she raised her voice and shouted, "Did you hear that, San Francisco? Today, Elizabeth Karen Kelly is thirty years old and ready to take on the world."

She smiled, feeling silly but also energized. She pulled out a pack of matches from her bag and lit the candle, holding her hand around the flame so the wind wouldn't blow it out while she was thinking of a wish.

As much as she wanted love, she was also scared of being vulnerable. She'd loved her father and he'd turned out to be a horrible person. She'd loved her mother and had been left behind. She'd picked Kyle because he was solid and stable and seemed like the anchor she needed in her life. But Kyle hadn't just held her down; he'd held her back.

If Prince Charming couldn't find her, perhaps she needed to find him. Drawing in a deep breath, she made a secret wish. *Someone for me to love*.

A gust of wind came up, blowing out the flame before she could do so. Probably a sign that her wish had not been heard. She felt an unexpected surge of disappointment.

That was the problem with hope… it made the fall back to reality even worse. She should know better. She pulled out the candle and licked the icing from it.

"Is that it?" a man asked.

She jumped at the unexpected voice, the cupcake flying out of her hand and over the side of the building. She stared in bemusement at the man who'd appeared out of nowhere. He was tall, with sandy blond hair, and was dressed in jeans, a white T-shirt with *Stanford* emblazoned across the front, and a brown leather jacket.

"You scared me," she said, her heart beating way too fast.

"Sorry." He gave her a smile. "So was that the extent of your celebration?"

"Uh." She glanced over the ledge, realizing her cupcake was long gone. "I guess so, since you made me drop my cake. What are you doing out here? Didn't you see the sign that said *Employees Only*?"

"I don't pay much attention to signs."

"So you're a rule breaker."

"When necessary. I needed some air. Sorry about the cupcake," he added.

"It was going to be really good, too," she said with a wistful sigh.

"How old are you today?"

"I'm thirty – the big three-O. I don't know why they call it that. It's not as if O stands for orgasm." Good grief. Had she said that out loud? For some reason, good-looking men made her jump into nervous conversation.

He gave her an odd look, probably wondering who would want to give her three orgasms.

She put up a hand. "Don't worry. I wasn't asking for volunteers."

"That wasn't what I was thinking."

"Yeah, right. You looked like a deer

caught in the headlights."

His smile widened. "Not true. So why are you out here by yourself on your birthday? You're too pretty not to have friends."

Her cheeks warmed as his gaze swept across her face and figure. She couldn't help wishing that she'd retouched her makeup, taken her brown hair out of its practical ponytail, and changed out of her loose, ill-fitting scrubs. Not that it mattered. She'd probably never see him again.

"Good line," she said. "You're a charmer."

"You don't like compliments."

"I don't like men who psychoanalyze me in the first five minutes of meeting me," she countered.

His grin broadened. "Got it. But you still haven't answered my question. Why the solo celebration?"

She didn't know why she felt the need to explain her pathetic party – maybe so it wouldn't look so pathetic. "My best friend just had a baby. Another one is on her honeymoon, and a third is home sick with the flu. I do have friends. They're just not available right now." Actually, her friends were rarely available these days. They'd moved on with their lives – getting married, having children – while she'd been treading water or trying to make things happen with Kyle. "And birthdays are not that big a deal," she added.

"I like birthdays. They're a good time to make a resolution."

"Isn't that what New Year's Eve is for?"

"Who says you can only make a resolution once a year?"

"No one, but I don't have much luck with the resolutions I do make. They usually involve losing twenty pounds, and so far I haven't managed to make that happen. I have a terrible chocolate addiction. If only they made a patch for that, I'd be set." *Great! Now she'd just pointed out that she needed to lose twenty pounds. No wonder she had trouble getting a man.*

"A resolution doesn't have to be about a diet," he said. "Last year I ran a marathon. The year before that I parachuted out of an airplane."

"Well, aren't you quite the hero." She wasn't sure if he was spinning her a line, but he certainly looked fit enough to run a marathon and young enough to taunt death by jumping out of an airplane. "What are you going to do this year?"

"Sail under the Golden Gate Bridge."

"That sounds like fun. When's the big day?"

"Tomorrow. But I'm much younger than you – I'm only turning twenty-nine."

"Ah, twenty-nine – I remember it well."

He laughed. "It was only what, twelve

hours ago?"

"About that. Do you know how to sail?"

"No. Will that be a problem?"

She couldn't help but smile back at him. His candor was refreshing, and she started to relax. "It might be. But something tells me you're pretty good at getting what you want."

"I used to be," he said, his tone turning somber. "I was the guy who had everything. Charmed."

"And charming."

He tipped his head. "I try."

"So what happened to that guy?"

"Life." A small sigh followed his words. Before she could ask what it meant, he added, "Are you a nurse here?"

"No, I just love to wear these baggy blue shirts and pants."

"Right. Stupid question." He paused. "How do you do it?"

"Do what?"

"Watch people die."

The change in subject surprised her. "Not everyone dies. Most people live."

"My father died here. It was long. Painful. Horrible. I'll never forget it."

She met his gaze head on. "I'm sorry."

"I bet you say that a lot."

"I still mean it." She knew what it was like to lose a parent. And it didn't matter how old you were.

"I was with my father when he passed.

He fought for months to recover, but he couldn't beat the cancer. Even though I knew the end was coming, and I was relieved that there would be an end to his pain and suffering, it was still shocking when it happened. One minute he was there, then he was gone…" He cleared his throat. "Hell of a birthday conversation. I apologize again."

"That's all right. Now I understand why you needed some air."

"The hospital smell sticks to my clothes. How do you take it?"

"You get used to it."

"Are you off duty?"

"Yes."

"Why don't I buy you a drink to toast your birthday?"

"Uh…" She didn't know what to say. It wasn't as if she had other plans, but he was a stranger.

"I promise, no more depressing conversation. We'll have a drink in honor of your new decade. I might even buy you another cake."

"I don't know you."

"That makes it better, doesn't it?" he said with a challenging smile. "You can let your hair down. Be whoever you want to be."

She had no idea who that person would be, but the idea was definitely appealing. Still, old habits died hard. "I should say no."

"Why?"

"Because it's not smart to go out with a perfect stranger. You could be an axe murderer or a serial killer or a life insurance salesman."

His deep, infectious laugh lit up the night, and his sparkling eyes made her feel like she'd been kicked in the stomach – or swept off her feet.

"I'm not any of those things."

"And you'd tell me if you were?"

"Good point, but isn't thirty about facing your fears? It's just a drink in a public place. Unless you're scared of a strawberry daiquiri?"

"Why would you *ever* think I would order a daiquiri?"

"Because you're too funny and honest to be the martini type."

"Which is what?"

"Sophisticated, brittle, phony laugh, dyed blonde hair, icy blue eyes, doesn't really give a damn about anyone but herself."

"That certainly rolled right off your tongue," she said, giving him a thoughtful look. "Why do I get the feeling you're describing someone in particular?"

"Guilty." He paused. "Get a drink with me and prove me wrong."

She hesitated. "I don't have anything to prove."

His gaze met hers and for some reason

she had the feeling he could read her mind. "Don't you?"

His challenge hung in the air for a long minute. Of course she had something to prove. She was going to change her life. And what better way to start than to do something she wouldn't normally do?

Besides that, she was intrigued by and attracted to this man, this stranger, who'd appeared out of nowhere. The idea crossed her mind that maybe he'd been sent to fulfill her birthday wish, but that was a foolish thought. He'd just lost his dad after a terrible illness. He'd come up to the roof to catch his breath. He hadn't come for her. It was purely coincidence.

"What's your name?" he asked.

She drew in a deep breath, feeling like she was about to cross over a line she couldn't cross back. But if she was ever going to take a chance, it might as well be now.

"Liz," she said. "My name is Liz. And I'd like that drink."

* * *

"Surprise! Happy birthday!"

Angela Payne stopped just inside the front door of her three-bedroom apartment in San Francisco's Sunset District. Smiling faces appeared from behind every piece of furniture, each one looking more sheepish than the next. She inwardly sighed. They should feel guilty. She'd told everyone that she didn't want a party to celebrate thirty-five. Time was not her friend, but her large Italian family turned every holiday or occasion into a party. The dining room table was laden with food, and music played loudly over the speakers. Judging by her Uncle Rico's red face, the wine was already flowing.

"I'm sorry. I tried to stop them," her husband Colin whispered as he kissed her on the cheek. "But your mother is a force of nature."

Looking at her five-foot-three-inch mother, Mary Margaret Razzini, no one would believe she was a force of anything, but her personality was much bigger than her stature. Angela had never yet won a battle where her mother was concerned, and she'd had far more practice than Colin.

Her mother lifted her chin, planted her hands on her waist, and said firmly, "It's your birthday, Angela. Of course you must have a party." She waved her hands in the air as she always did when she spoke. "I made three kinds of lasagna. You'll eat, you'll laugh, and you'll have fun. Mama knows best." Her mother turned her head sharply as one of the grandchildren tugged on her skirt. "Yes, yes, Jimmy. I will get you some lemonade." She headed off to the kitchen, as if she owned the place.

"I'll help her," Colin said quickly, disappearing before she could remind him that the only request she'd made for her birthday was to have a private dinner with him. She had things she wanted to discuss, but not in front of her family.

"Try the shrimp cheese puffs," Lisa said, holding up a silver tray. "I made them myself."

She stared down at her petite, dark-haired sister and gave her a glare. "I told you I didn't want a party."

"It makes Mama happy to take care of you. She's been so lost since Daddy died."

"Daddy died nine years ago. When are you going to stop offering that excuse for everything Mama does that we don't like?"

"She still misses him," Lisa said with a shrug. "Try one of my puffs."

Angela popped a shrimp cheese puff into her mouth. It was hot, tangy, and delicious. "Not bad."

"Not bad?" Lisa echoed in annoyance. "They're spectacular. And who are you to criticize, anyway? You can't even make good spaghetti sauce. You're lucky Colin can cook, or you'd starve to death."

She smiled at her younger sister's predictable reaction. Pushing Lisa's insecurity button was an old habit and probably one she should have outgrown by now. "I was just kidding. The puff is fabulous." It was true that she couldn't cook like her two sisters and her mother. But then, she'd always been the odd one out, a tall, blue-eyed blonde in a sea of dark-eyed brunettes, some latent gene from her grandmother. She preferred painting to cooking. She was the artist in the family, the one who lost track of time while sketching a picture, the one who had no domestic talents. Fortunately, her husband didn't mind cooking or eating take-out.

"I also made the cannelloni," Lisa added, waving her hand toward the dining room table where most of the party was gathered. "It's better than Gina's, but don't tell her I told you that."

"Believe me, I won't." Gina and Lisa had competed with each other for as long as she could remember, and she'd always been caught in the middle, each one wanting her to take their side. "David must count his lucky stars every day that he married you," she said, popping another puff into her mouth. She waved to David, who was sitting on the couch with one of his two children on his lap. His belly hung over his belt, a definite sign that he'd been sampling more than a few of Lisa's puffs.

"David is driving me crazy," her sister confided. "He wants me to have another baby, as if we don't have our hands full with the ones that we–" She bit off the end of her sentence, her brown eyes darkening. "Sorry, Angie."

"It's fine," she said quickly, not wanting to get into that subject.

"It's not fine, and I shouldn't have said anything."

"What's going on?" Gina asked, interrupting their conversation. She handed Angela a glass of wine. "What's the look on your face about? You can't possibly be that mad about the party."

She really didn't want to talk to Gina tonight. Whereas Lisa was insecure about her choices, her older sister Gina was always right. She had a strong personality and never had any trouble expressing her opinions, which made her a very good lawyer but not the nicest person to be around.

"Would it matter if I was?" she asked.

"Mama is the one who gave birth to you. If she wants to celebrate your birthday, you should smile and say thank you," Gina told her. "She went through eighteen hours of labor to bring you into the world. That was no picnic."

Her gut tightened. No matter what conversation she seemed to be in, it always came down to babies. "I have to wash my hands," she muttered.

As she walked away, she could hear Lisa telling Gina how stupid she was to bring up the subject of their mother giving birth, and Gina replying, "For God's sake, doesn't Angela ever think about anyone but herself?"

This was exactly why she hadn't wanted a party. She loved her family, but lately she couldn't stand being around them. Her sisters and cousins were all married. They had children. Some even had teenagers. She was so far behind the curve it was ridiculous. She was jealous. She knew it. They knew it, too.

In the bathroom, she closed the door and stared at her face in the mirror. She'd never imagined she'd be thirty-five and without a baby. But three attempts at in-vitro fertilization had left her with an empty womb and a bankrupt savings account. Time was running out. She might have only one more chance. Colin had recently received a big bonus at work, and she knew just how she wanted to spend the money. She had hoped to talk to him about it tonight, but that would have to wait until they were alone. She certainly didn't want any input from her mother or her sisters.

She washed her hands, splashed water on her face, and reapplied her lipstick. She was too thin, too pale. She'd always had a tendency to wear her stress on her face and today it was all there. She forced a smile. She just had to get through the next few hours. Her family had gone to a lot of trouble for her. She had to at least pretend to be happy. As Gina said, it wasn't always about her.

Leaving the bathroom, she walked

down the hall and into the dining room. Colin was filling a plate at the buffet table. At forty, her husband could still make her heart skip a beat. He was a very attractive man, tall and lean, with light brown hair and golden brown eyes. He'd taken off his suit jacket, loosened his tie, and rolled the sleeves of his white dress shirt up to his elbows. His hair was mussed. He had a habit of running his fingers through it whenever he was tired or worried. She could always tell what kind of day he'd had by the way his hair looked. Tonight it was a mess, probably because her mother had railroaded him into throwing her a surprise birthday party.

Turning, he caught her watching him and gave her an apologetic smile. "I made this for you, Angie."

She walked over and took the plate out of his hands. "Thanks."

He handed her a fork. "No knife for you. I'm afraid you'll use it on me."

"Good thinking."

"Your family loves you so much. They wanted to make you happy. I got swept up in their enthusiasm. By the time your mother finished talking to me, I was convinced that throwing you a surprise party was the best idea in the world, until you walked through the door a few minutes ago."

"It's okay. Your intentions were good." She looked around the crowded apartment, knowing she was lucky and blessed. "Everyone wants me to be happy, including you, and I have an idea about that."

"So do I. Come with me." Colin led her into the kitchen, which was surprisingly empty. He took an envelope out of the drawer and handed it to her. "This is your real birthday surprise."

Her pulse leapt with expectation. "What's this?"

"Your present. I've been thinking about what to do with that bonus I got from work, and I came up with the perfect idea."

"Me, too," she said, meeting his gaze. "I wanted to talk to you about it tonight. It seems like fate that your bonus is exactly the amount we need to..." She opened the envelope, expecting to see a letter with an appointment time at the fertility clinic, like so many they'd received in the past. Instead, she saw tickets – tickets to some sort of cruise.

"The Caribbean," Colin said with excitement in his voice. "Ten days cruising the high seas, just you and me. Miles of ocean, music, casino action, and all the food you can eat. It will be a second honeymoon, a new start. We can talk about what we want to do with the rest of our lives."

"You spent your bonus on a cruise?" she asked in shock.

"Yes. Why?" His smiled dimmed. "What's wrong, Angie?"

She looked into his eyes, wondering how he could possibly be confused about her reaction. "I thought we would use the money to try IVF one more time. It's the exact amount we need."

The blood drained out of his face. His jaw tightened. "We agreed that we were done after the last time."

"We didn't agree. We just ran out of money. But now we have the money."

He shook his head. "It's not about the money. It's about you and me. I can't watch you go through it again. I can't see the hope in your eyes and then the despair. I'm afraid one of these days you'll break, and I won't be able to put you back together. Some things are not meant to be. We have to accept it."

"The doctor still thinks it could happen for us. I'm only thirty-five. There's still time – but not a lot of time. Each year the odds go down."

"You hear what you want to hear. The doctor told you it might never happen, Angie."

"He also said it might," she argued. "How can you give up?"

He put his hands on her shoulders, gazing into her eyes. "We're happy, aren't we? We love each other. We have good friends, family, nieces and nephews to spoil. You have your gallery, your painting. Why can't that be enough for you?"

"Because it can't." She stepped away from him, unable to bear his touch. He was trying to take away her dreams.

"You have to be realistic–"

"No, I need to have a baby. And I don't want to look back in five years and say, What if I had just tried one more time? Don't you think we owe it to ourselves to take one last chance?"

He stared at her for a long moment. She wanted to see him weaken, watch the reassuring smile come into his eyes and spread across his face. She wanted him to say, "Yes, that's what I want, too."

"I can't."

His words didn't register for a moment, but slowly they sank in. His expression was definite, unyielding. God! *He wasn't going to change his mind.* A feeling of desperation swept over her. *Was this it? Was this really the end?*

If Colin wouldn't agree to the insemination, they were done. It was over. She would never have a baby. She would never feel that tiny life inside her. She pressed her hand to her empty womb, an ache spreading down deep in her soul.

She'd touched her sisters' pregnant stomachs many times, feeling the kicks and flutters of their babies, and she'd wanted that incredible and special feeling inside her own body. She'd always thought she'd have that moment. The idea that she wouldn't was too much to handle. She felt like she couldn't breathe, as though the walls were closing in on her.

"It will get easier," Colin told her, a hint of desperation in his voice. "We'll fill up our days. We'll make ourselves happy. It will be all right."

Before she could say anything else, the kitchen door flew open and her mother walked in, holding a cake lit up with candles. Her sisters, their husbands, their children, and the rest of the party crowded into the small kitchen.

She stared down at the cake, the blaze of thirty-five candles surrounding the words *Happy Birthday Angela*.

"Make a wish," her mother said, setting the cake down on the table in front of her.

She had tried wishing. It didn't work. But everyone was waiting. They were calling out suggestions for wishes… *A new car… A trip around the world.* They were suffocating her with their desire to have her move on, give up her dream and wish for something that wouldn't take a miracle. Then they could go on, too. They wouldn't have to watch what they said or worry about her.

She had to give them what they wanted. It was what she always did.

But when she closed her eyes to make her secret wish there was only one thought in her mind.

Please, God, give me a baby.

She blew out the candles to applause and laughter and an off-key version of *Happy Birthday*. Her mother suggested they take the cake back out to the dining room to cut it, and Angela was grateful when the group moved out of the kitchen, leaving her and Colin alone again.

He gave her a pleading look, silently begging her to stop arguing, to accept what was done. "Let's get some cake," he said. "It's your favorite."

"I'm not hungry."

Her Uncle Rico popped back into the room. "We need more wine, Colin. Time for the secret stash every good Italian keeps down in the cellar."

"I don't have a secret stash or a cellar," Colin said. "But the liquor store down the street has plenty of wine."

"I'll go." Angela grabbed the excuse like a lifeline. She had to get out of this room, out of this party, out of this life.

"You can't leave – it's your party. I'll go," Colin said.

"No, I need some air."

He frowned, obviously unhappy with her decision. "What do you want me to tell your mother?"

"Tell her I've had all the surprises I can take for one night."

"Angela."

"What?"

"Don't take too long."

"I'm just going to get wine," she said. "How long could that take?"

Chapter Two

Liz felt an excited shiver run down her spine as she stepped out of a cab in front of the thirty-story glass building that housed one of San Francisco's newest luxury downtown hotels, the Remington. She still couldn't believe she'd hopped into a taxi with a perfect stranger who was intent on buying her an expensive glass of champagne. It felt more like a scene from a movie than real life – at least, not her real life.

"After you," John said, waving her toward the revolving doors.

She hesitated. "Are you sure you don't want to go somewhere else? Neither one of us is dressed for this place." She'd changed out of her scrubs into a pair of blue jeans, a knit shirt, and a black sweater, her usual out-of-work clothes, which were definitely not high class, sophisticated, or even unwrinkled, for that matter, having been stuffed in her locker all day.

"It's your birthday. You deserve the best," he said.

"You're right, I do deserve the best," she said slowly. It was not the way she usually thought about her life, but maybe it

was time she did. "I might have to find an
ATM first, though."

"This is my treat."

"I'm used to paying my own way."

"Tonight you don't have to. Don't
worry, I can afford it."

"I'd feel better if you told me a little
more about yourself, including your last
name." So far, he'd only provided her with
John. And she wasn't even sure that was his
real name. There'd been something odd in
his voice, another reminder that she was
taking a risk by going out with him, but
she'd been playing it safe for so long that
she was ready to shake things up.

"I don't think we should exchange last
names," he said with a grin. "It will make
tonight more fun."

She wanted to argue, but it was just a
drink, for God's sake. She didn't need two
forms of ID to accept a glass of champagne,
did she?

"Come on, Liz, let's start the
celebration. You're not getting any
younger," he teased.

"Fine. No last names."

John took her hand as they headed
toward the door. His touch made her feel
warm all over. She couldn't remember the
last time she'd held hands with a man. Kyle
had hated holding her hand. He'd said that
he felt constrained. That had probably been
a clue that he was not going to want a future

with her if he couldn't even hold her hand, but she'd overlooked that clue along with plenty of others in her desperation to be as attached as everyone else in her circle of friends.

As they entered the hotel, she couldn't help but be impressed by the cathedral ceilings, the marble floors, and the glass chandeliers. The people walking through the lobby were just as pretty, the men in designer suits, the women in expensive evening gowns. If there had been a red carpet, she might have thought they were at the Oscars or a movie premiere where everyone was someone.

She'd been someone once – someone famous – but not in a good way. And she'd felt immensely relieved when her fifteen minutes of fame had elapsed.

John led the way up an escalator to the second floor. She assumed he was heading for the bar until he stopped in the doorway of a ballroom, which was jammed with at least a few hundred people.

"What is it – a wedding?" she asked, trying to peer around his shoulder.

"Looks like a birthday party." He tipped his head toward a poster on an easel by the door. "Carole Prescott's fortieth birthday party. Hey, she shares your birthday. I think it's a sign."

"Of course it's a sign, John. That's what they call words on big posters."

"Funny girl. I mean a sign that we're in the right place." A mischievous glint came into his eyes. "We should join the party."

"No way. We can't go in there. We don't even know her. You said a glass of champagne in the bar."

"I bet they have champagne here." John squeezed her hand and pulled her into the darkened room while she was still protesting. She waited for someone to kick them out immediately, but everyone's attention was focused on the far end of the room, where a huge, three-tiered cake decorated with multicolored roses had been rolled into the center of the dance floor.

"Look at that," John muttered. "It's big enough to feed a small country."

It was certainly bigger than the cupcake she'd bought. "That must have cost a fortune."

"Kind of puts your little party of one to shame, doesn't it?"

"Hey, just because a party is small doesn't mean it's not good," she protested, but she was lying, and they both knew it. Who wouldn't want a celebration like this?

"I think there's going to be a speech," he said.

Liz watched as a distinguished man in a black tuxedo escorted an equally stunning blonde in a turquoise beaded evening dress to the nearby microphone.

"Before we light the candles," the man

said, "I'd like to make a toast to my incredible wife, Carole." He picked up two glasses of champagne from an attending waiter and handed one to the woman by his side. "You're an amazing wife and mother. You're tireless in your efforts to take care of your family and others. You've given me an incredible seventeen years of marriage and two beautiful children. I'm the luckiest man on the face of the earth. Happy birthday." He kissed her on the lips as the crowd murmured "Happy birthday" and raised their champagne glasses.

It was a beautiful, loving toast, Liz thought, watching as two waiters began to light the candles. It took a few minutes to get all forty lit. When they did, it looked like a royal bonfire. She'd never seen such a spectacular sight. Carole Prescott was a very lucky woman.

For a moment she tried to imagine that this was her party, that the man in the black tuxedo was her husband, that the guests were all there for her. But her mind came up blank. Her imagination wasn't that good.

As Carole stepped toward the cake, her gaze ran around the room, settling on Liz and John. She frowned.

"Uh-oh," Liz whispered.

"Time to go," John said. They ran to the door like two kids who'd been caught sneaking into the movies. They didn't stop running until they reached the bar.

Laughing, they grabbed a booth in the corner. It took a moment for Liz to catch her breath. She hadn't felt this alive in a long time. "I have a feeling you are going to be a bad influence on me."

"That's funny. Because I was just thinking that you might be a very good influence on me," John replied.

"What does that mean?"

"Maybe I'll tell you – before the night is through."

* * *

If Carole Prescott could have skipped any birthday, it would have been this one.

She didn't want to be forty. She didn't want to deal with the ugliness of aging and the fear that her husband would find someone younger and prettier. She didn't want to get left behind. And she was terribly afraid that could happen.

Her husband, Blake, had big ambitions. He was a high-profile corporate attorney who wanted to be a United States senator, and he'd used the occasion of her birthday to network and raise funds for his upcoming political campaign. More than half the people in the room were here for him. They didn't give a damn about her birthday. But they'd smile and pretend to care, and she'd do the same. It was what she always did.

She couldn't complain. She'd chosen

this life. She'd worked hard to get it. And she'd never allowed herself to look back or regret any of her choices…until tonight.

While she normally loved parties and being the center of attention, she would have preferred not to have this particular party. She didn't want to mark this day, have the society columnists shouting to the world that Carole Prescott was forty years old. It would only mean more scrutiny in the future and gossip about whether or not she'd had a face lift, Botox, or plastic surgery.

It was different for men. Her husband loved being forty. For him, aging gave him life experience and wisdom, the perfect combination for a senator. But what did aging give her but a time bomb ticking down the days to the end of her life?

She was being dramatic, but it was her nature. She'd always wanted to live bigger than life. From the time she was a little girl living in a seedy, run-down apartment building, she'd believed that some day she would be somebody. And she *was* somebody. She'd just had no idea how difficult and wearying it would be to wear a mask of perfection twenty-four hours a day. She could never relax, kick off her shoes, let down her hair, put on old sweats and dance around the living room the way her mother used to do every single night after waiting tables at the local burger restaurant.

Not that she wanted her mother's life –

God, no! She'd done everything she could to get away from that world.

As the crowd chanted *Make a wish! Make a wish!* Carole closed her eyes, trying to shake off the past and focus on the present, the future. It was difficult to concentrate. The noise from the crowd made her head spin and the heat from the candles drew beads of sweat along her forehead. All she could see in her mind was the past in bright, living color, reminding her of who she'd once been and what she'd left behind.

There were eight candles on her cake. Her mom wore her flashy red hair in a ponytail and there was a cigarette hanging out of her smiling mouth. Her aunt held a cheap disposable camera in her hand. The other kids crowded around the scratched-up picnic table in the city park. Alex, who lived across the hall, asked for one of the red roses on the cake. His younger brother, Peter, wiped his hand across his face, smearing the mustard and ketchup from the hot dog he'd eaten from ear to ear. They kept shoving each other, trying to get the best spot on the bench.

Her friend, Becky, slipped her hand into Carole's and asked if she could help blow out the candles. Becky always wanted to do everything Carole did, especially when it came to presents and candles. Not that there were many presents, just a doll from the dollar store and paper and crayons to draw with.

Her mom had written Happy B'day Carly in red frosting that was jagged and barely readable. Carly was what everyone called her. Her mom said she'd named her Carole for her grandmother, but it was too big a name for a little girl.

"Make a wish, baby, a secret wish that comes straight from your heart," her mom said. "And make it a good one. Lord knows we need all the wishes we can get."

Because they didn't have much more than wishes, she thought. She was only eight, but she knew that with a certainty that would have surprised her mom and her aunt, who tried to whisper when they talked about the fact that her dad, Billy, had run out on 'em, taking all their money and all their dreams. She was glad he was gone. She didn't miss her dad or the beer bottles in the fridge or the Saturday night fights that made her mom cry and wear long-sleeved shirts all weekend. She tried to take care of her mother and keep the house clean, but her daddy seemed to get mad anyway.

Her mom always said, "Don't worry, Carly, Mama's got your back," but it wasn't the truth. Sometimes her mother wasn't there when her daddy came home mad.

She closed her eyes, trying not to think about him, and wished for a big house, piles of money, and plenty of milk for her and her mom. They liked to dunk Oreo cookies into the milk when they watched TV at night.

Certain that she had the right wish, she opened her eyes to blow out the candles just in time to see Alex push Peter so hard he fell headfirst into the cake, setting his hair on fire. He started screaming along with everyone else.

Suddenly everyone at the party was blowing on the cake, making sure all the flames were out and Peter was okay. That stupid Alex had ruined her party.

She looked down at her smashed cake and had a feeling her wish would never come true. She burst into tears and her mom's arms came around her in a tight and loving hug.

"Don't worry, Carly. The birthday fairy already heard your wish. It will come true. You're a special girl, and God takes care of special little girls."

Her mother had been right. Her wish had come true. She had a big house, piles of money, and plenty of milk. Only she didn't drink milk anymore – it was too fattening. And she didn't share her house or her life with her mother. For the first time in a long time, she missed her mom. She missed her children, too. She couldn't see them anywhere in the crowd.

Her husband told her to hurry up and make a wish before the candles burned down. An unexpected wish filled her heart. *I want my family back.*

As she opened her eyes and blew out the candles, she regretted her foolish wish. Her family hadn't gone anywhere. Her family was her husband and her children. So what had she been wishing for?

But as she stepped away from the cake so the waiters could begin serving, she couldn't shake the feeling of hollowness. She had everything and yet it felt like nothing.

The band began to play softly in the background, and she realized she was standing alone in the lingering smoke from her candles. How was that possible? The birthday girl wasn't supposed to be alone.

She needed to move, join a group and make small talk. She was good at cocktail conversation. Blake had always admired the way she could work a room. But she didn't feel like working the room tonight. Her stiletto heels were pinching her toes, and her facial muscles were tired of smiling. At the very least, she needed to sit down for a few minutes and catch a second wind before the band started playing. There would be dancing and more toasts to endure. She had to find her party spirit – and fast.

"Mrs. Prescott, are you all right?" Lindsay, the party coordinator, a perky blonde in her early thirties, had a clipboard in her hand and a worried look on her face.

"I'm fine. The party is lovely. You did a wonderful job. Thank you."

The tension in Lindsay's face eased. "You're very welcome. I hope you're having a good time."

"Yes, of course. Have you seen my children around?"

"They left right before you cut the cake. Your daughter told me that she was driving your son to a sleepover or something like that. I assumed you knew their plans."

She'd known they'd each made plans to spend the night somewhere else since she and Blake had booked a room at the hotel, but beyond that she knew very little. She was disappointed that they'd left so early. They hadn't even wanted to watch her cut the cake. They hadn't wanted to do much of anything with her in recent years. She'd attributed their distance to the teenage years – Sophie was sixteen now and Michael was fifteen. They had their own lives.

But she knew the distance between them had started years earlier. Her devotion to Blake and his career had forced her to miss some of the children's events. Blake needed her to host parties, to travel with him, to support his career, and she'd always believed that helping him achieve his goals would give her children a better life. And it had. They lived in a big house. Her kids had nice clothes, the latest electronics and computers. They lacked for nothing, and that was because of her effort. Still, deep in her heart, she missed having a real relationship with them.

Well, maybe she hadn't been the best mother, but she was a fabulous wife. That she had no doubts about.

Speaking of being a wife, maybe it was time to find her husband.

She strolled through the ballroom, keeping a sharp eye out for Blake. As the minutes passed, she grew more and more annoyed by his absence. Lately, he never seemed to be around. She didn't mind being in his shadow, as long as he was actually near enough to cast one.

The party had spilled out into the hallways that ran along the ballroom. She smiled and waved to several guests as she searched the halls for Blake. She turned the far corner, wondering if he'd gone into the kitchen or one of the banquet offices to speak to someone. She thought the corridor was empty until she saw a couple almost hidden by a tall plant.

She stopped abruptly, recognizing the broad shoulders of her husband. The woman with him had long red hair and she wore a very short black strapless dress. She couldn't have been more than twenty-five years old.

As Carole watched, the redhead leaned in and whispered something in Blake's ear. Then she slid her lips along his cheekbone. The intimate gesture was unmistakable.

Carole's stomach turned over and her

heart skipped a beat. Oh, God! Was this it, then? Was her husband already having an affair with a younger woman?

She must have let out some kind of sound, because suddenly Blake whirled around and saw her. His eyes glittered the way they always did when he was nervous or guilty. The woman with him didn't appear worried at all. She looked triumphant, as if she'd just won some big prize.

"Carole," he muttered, walking toward her. "Have you met Krystal Cunningham? Her father just made a very large donation to my campaign."

She heard the explanation. She didn't believe it. She wanted to stamp her foot and scream at him that he was a liar and a stupid one at that, to fool around with this woman at his wife's birthday party. But she couldn't do any of those things. She couldn't make a scene. That wasn't who she was, or who she wanted to be. So she said, "I see. And you were just thanking her."

"Exactly."

She saw the relief in his eyes, the acknowledgement that they would both handle this with dignity and poise. Her hands clenched into fists. She had the tremendous urge to give him a hard, stinging slap across that handsome face, to shake him up, to make him realize that she wasn't doing this for him, she was doing it for herself. The last role she wanted to play was the pitiful, betrayed wife at her own party.

"It's nice to meet you, Mrs. Prescott," Krystal said in a voice that almost purred. "I hope you don't mind me borrowing your husband for a few moments. I find his thoughts on politics so intriguing."

Carole wanted to slap her, too. Ignoring Krystal, she said, " I'll see you inside, Blake." She turned and walked quickly back the way she'd come, her heart beating in double time, fury boiling her blood. She wasn't sure if Blake was having an affair or just participating in a dangerous flirtation. Either way, he was stepping over the line. She'd never believed he would risk damaging his reputation with a sexual fling. Maybe she was wrong.

She suddenly had doubts about him and everything else in her life. It was this damn birthday making her want to re-evaluate her choices. And she was terribly afraid that if she looked too closely, she'd see nothing – no substance, no meaning, just pretty things, pretty people, and pretty lies.

Making a decision that was probably reckless and foolish, she bypassed the ballroom and headed for the escalator. She had a desperate urge to get the hell away from the party.

Her walk turned into a jog, then a dead run as she ran down the escalator, through the lobby, and toward the front door of the hotel.

Was that her husband calling her name?

She pushed through the revolving door and stepped onto the sidewalk. The valet gave her a curious look. She ignored him, spotting her limousine across the street.

She was so intent on getting away from the party that she didn't realize there was any traffic. The shocking glare of headlights made her freeze in the middle of the street. She saw a car bearing down her... just a second too late.

* * *

Angela slammed on the brakes and held onto the wheel as her car skidded down the road, finally coming to a crashing stop just inches away from a beautiful blonde woman in an evening dress. For a moment all she could do was try to catch her breath. Her hands were shaking as she took them off the steering wheel. Then she unfastened her seat belt and stepped onto the street. "Are you all right?"

The woman didn't reply. She looked as if she were in shock and frozen in place. Her blue eyes were wide and glassy.

"You're not hurt. I didn't hit you," Angela said, trying to reassure herself as much as anyone.

The valet from the hotel joined them,

asking if anyone needed help.

The woman finally woke up. She muttered, "No, I'm fine." Then she ran across the street and jumped into the back of a white limousine.

"Carole," a man called, running out of the hotel. "Come back. Damn," he swore as the limousine pulled away.

Angela glanced at the man in the tuxedo, wondering if he was the reason the woman had run into the street without looking. A honking horn reminded her that her car was blocking traffic. With her heart still racing, she returned to the car, started the engine, and pulled away.

She could have hit that woman – maybe even killed her – and all in the matter of a few seconds. Thank goodness it hadn't gone that way. She supposed she should offer up a prayer of gratitude, but she doubted anyone would be listening. The last eight years had certainly tried her once unshakeable faith.

Her cell phone rang for the third time since she'd left the apartment. She couldn't ignore it again. Pulling over to the curb so she wouldn't almost run into anyone else, she flipped open the phone and said, "Hello."

"Angie, where are you?" Colin asked worriedly. "You've been gone for almost an hour."

She thought it had only been a few

minutes since she'd left the house to get wine. But she realized now she'd been driving around for a while. "I'm sorry. I got distracted." She paused. "I don't think I'm going to come back for a while. You better go out and get Uncle Rico his wine."

"What are you doing, Angela?"

"Taking a drive. I need some time to think."

"Come back here and think. I'll send everyone home. We'll sit down and talk."

"Are you going to change your mind?"

Her question was met with tense silence. "No," he said finally. "I could lie and tell you I'd think about it, but it wouldn't be the truth. And we love each other too much to lie."

He was right. The time had come to put all their cards on the table. "I don't think I'm going to change my mind either, Colin. I'll be home later. Don't wait up for me."

"It's your birthday. Of course I'm going to wait up for you."

"That's right, it's my birthday. I'm thirty-five years old. I can take care of myself." She ended the call before he could say anything else. She loved Colin, but right now he was standing between her and the baby she'd always wanted. She hated him for that. Why couldn't he try one more time? It wasn't as if it were his body going through the painful injections of hormones.

She put the car back into gear and drove

down the street. As she stopped at a light, she suddenly realized where she was – North Beach, the neighborhood she'd grown up in. The church where she and the rest of her Italian Catholic family went to Mass every Sunday was just down the block. She hadn't been to Mass with the family in a couple of years. She'd told her mother and sisters that she and Colin were going to a new church closer to their house, but the truth was that they weren't going to any church.

The light turned green and she drove past the tall, massive building with the steeples and spires and found herself hitting the brake once again. She pulled into a spot nearby and shut off the engine. It was doubtful that the church would even be open on a Friday night. But maybe… maybe she'd just see. It was time she and God had a little chat.

* * *

Carole sat back against the cushy limo seat, her body shaking, her breath coming hard and fast. She'd almost been run over. If that woman hadn't stopped her car in time, she'd be dead right now. God! *She'd be dead.* Forty years old and gone. She'd imagined dying a million times but it had never been like that – so sudden, so fast, and so irrevocable.

Someone had been watching out for her. She'd been given another chance.

To do what? She had a feeling she was supposed to know the answer to that question, but she didn't. She was in new territory tonight. She'd done something she'd never done before: run out on her own life.

Actually, that wasn't completely true. She'd run away once before, on her twentieth birthday. She'd left the old neighborhood behind. She'd turned her back on friends and family to go after her dream.

And now she was running away again.

There would be repercussions. Blake would be furious. The guests would wonder where she was and why she'd left so abruptly. There would be speculation about whether she was sick, or if she'd drunk too much, or if – God forbid – she'd seen another woman kissing her husband. Greta Sorenson, San Francisco's society columnist, would probably gossip about her sudden departure in tomorrow's edition of the *Tribune.* She really needed to go back to the party.

It wasn't too late. She'd only been gone a few minutes. She could laugh off her disappearance with some smooth explanation about fixing a broken strap on her high heel or something like that. The only problem was… she didn't want to go back.

How could that be? How could she suddenly not want what she'd always wanted?

Reaching into the liquor cabinet, she pulled out a bottle of Jack Daniels and a shot glass. She filled it to the brim and then tossed the liquid down her throat. It tingled and burned, making her feel like she was really alive. After the second shot, she felt calmer.

She glanced out the window, watching the city go by. She loved San Francisco, loved its changing neighborhoods, foggy nights, and windswept views of the bay and the ocean. She'd spent her entire life in this city – a city of many cultures and neighborhoods that changed from one block to the next. For the first twenty years of her life, she'd called a low-income housing project in Potrero Hill home, and for the last twenty years, she'd resided in the expensive Marina District. She'd lived two lives. And now she was wondering where the next twenty years would take her.

It shocked her that she had no real idea of what was supposed to come next. From the time she was a little girl, she'd always been focused, driven. Every step she'd taken had been deliberate, purposeful, with one goal – to change her life for the better. She'd hated the run-down one-bedroom apartment she'd shared with her mother after her father took off. She'd hated the lumpy single mattress on the floor in the corner of the living room that had been her bed for so many years. She'd hated feeling like she wasn't good enough. So every night, she'd looked out at the bright downtown city lights and imagined a different world.

She'd made a plan to get an education, find a job and a better place to live, marry well and have children who would never have to grow up the way she had. And she'd done it all. She'd been ruthless and a little selfish. She was honest enough with herself to admit that, although she doubted she'd admit it to anyone else. She'd carefully cultivated an image, and very few people really knew her – certainly none of the people who had been at her birthday party.

She hadn't thought about her childhood in a very long time, and as she settled back in her seat, some good moments flashed through her head. They hadn't had money, but she had been very close to her mom – the two of them against the world, her mom used to say. But her mother hadn't really wanted out of that world, or if she had, she hadn't had the courage or the determination to get out. So Carole had gone without her.

Sighing, she poured herself another shot of whiskey and drank it down. Even if she found peace in the liquor, it wouldn't last long. She'd tried that before, more than a few times.

"Mrs. Prescott?" The chauffeur's voice

came over the speaker. "Shall I take you home now?"

She suddenly realized that the chauffeur had been doing exactly what she'd requested: driving around.

"Yes," she whispered. "I want to go home." But not to the mansion that overlooked the Golden Gate Bridge. She pushed the intercom again. "Potrero Hill," she said. "I'll give you more specific directions when we get there."

Leaning back against the seat, she hoped she hadn't just made the second worst decision of the night.

Chapter Three

Angela walked up the steps to St. Catherine's Church. The front door was locked. She tried the side doors, but they were also locked. There were lights on in the nearby rectory where the priests resided, but she didn't want to go that far. The fact that the church was closed seemed prophetic. She was on her own in every possible way. She didn't know why she'd bothered to stop.

"Can I help you?"

She whirled around in surprise at the sound of a male voice – and a familiar one at that. The tall, fair-haired man with the light blue eyes and the smattering of freckles across his nose had once been her very best friend and the object of a teenage crush. Now he'd traded his blue jeans and T-shirts for black slacks, a black shirt and a priest's collar.

"Patrick O'Brien," she said with a disbelieving shake of her head. She and Patrick had gone to Catholic school together until the eleventh grade, when his family had moved away. She remembered her mother telling her that Patrick had become a priest, but she hadn't realized he was working here at St. Catherine's. She wondered why her mother hadn't told her that. Or maybe she had. Lately, Angela tried to avoid any conversations about old friends from the neighborhood. The stories usually involved someone getting married or having another baby.

"Angela Razzini," Patrick said with the same boyish grin that had once made her heart tumble over in her chest. "It's about time you dropped by."

"It's Angela Payne now. I'm married."

"Your mother said you were."

"Oh, that's right. I guess you must see her a lot."

"Every Sunday. As well as your sisters, their spouses, and their children. But no Angela, never Angela. Why is that?" he asked with a thoughtful smile.

"I live on the other side of town."

"So it's a question of geography?"

She hesitated, wondering how bad it would be to lie to a priest, even if she had once swapped peanut butter and jelly sandwiches with him. "How long have you been here?" she asked instead.

"Six months. I was in L.A. for a while, but San Francisco is home. How have you been?"

"Great. I've been great."

He smiled in that way that priests do when they know you're not telling the truth. "Is that why you're trying to get into my church on a Friday night?"

"It was an impulse. I was driving by, I saw the church, and I started thinking about the past."

"Of course," he said with a knowing nod. "It's your birthday, a good time for reflection."

"How on earth did you remember that?" she asked in amazement.

"I remember a lot of things about you, Angie, like your smile and the way it lit up your face when you got excited about something. You made all the kids feel good, including me. And you had such a passion for your art. You used to paint on every available space – the back of your parents' garage, my bedroom wall, and even Mrs. Murphy's fence. She did not appreciate your artwork, however," he added with a laugh.

"That's true. I thought she was going to put a curse on me." The old woman had lived in the corner house that all the neighborhood kids thought was haunted. They'd been convinced she was a witch. One boring summer day Patrick had dared her to draw a picture on the back fence, and she'd sketched a witch flying over the moon on a broomstick. Mrs. Murphy had been furious. Angela had been grounded for a month, not to mention having to go to confession, say hundreds of *Hail Marys*, and write a letter of apology. "You made me do that," she said, pointing her finger at him, "and I was the one who got into trouble as usual."

"You were a loyal friend. You didn't rat me out. I appreciated that." He paused. "Do you still paint?"

"Not as much as I used to, but I have a small art gallery in Noe Valley. I show the work of local artists."

"I'll have to stop by. Do you sell any of your own work?"

"Not lately." She hadn't been inspired to paint during the last few years. That part of her body seemed to have dried up along with everything else.

"I'm not surprised you own your own business. You always inspired me with your determination to succeed, to get what you wanted."

"Sometimes it takes more than determination." *Sometimes it takes a miracle.* But she couldn't say that to him. He was a priest. Although who better than a priest to get her that miracle?

"Sometimes it does," he agreed. "I've always found prayer to be helpful."

"Always?" she asked, unable to keep the doubt out of her voice. "I never thought you would become a priest, Patrick. You loved trouble."

He laughed. "Hey, I wasn't that bad, and we went to Catholic school together. I was an altar boy."

"I never thought that you, of all people, could live a life free of sin. You certainly had some sinful ideas when we were kids – like the frog in Mr. Martin's suit pocket and the time we took the tops off the salt shakers at the Snack Shack."

"Innocent childhood pranks," he said with a grin. "I grew up, confessed my sins, did penance, and now I try to do better. God helps me."

"Lucky you," she muttered, reminded of why she'd stopped here in the first place.

"What kind of man did you marry? Is he good to you?"

"Yes. He's in advertising. I met him when I worked for an agency doing graphic design. That was ten years ago. His name is Colin."

"And where is he tonight – on your birthday?" His eyes grew speculative, and she remembered that she'd always had trouble lying to Patrick. He had a way of seeing straight into her heart. That trait probably made him a very good priest. At the moment, it just made her feel uncomfortable.

"He's at home. My family decided to throw me a surprise party after I told them not to."

"You used to like surprises. What happened?"

"Thirty-five happened. This birthday reminds me of what I don't have." She shook her head, feeling the emotions beginning to well up inside her. "I should go."

"Don't run away. You came here for a reason. Tell me what's going on."

"I didn't come here on purpose."

"But you still got here. Do you want to go inside?" He pulled a key ring out of his black slacks. "I can give you a few minutes alone. Maybe you want to say a prayer."

She thought about his offer and decided against it. "There's nothing for me inside the church."

"Are you sure?"

His blue eyes were both curious and compassionate, and she found herself wanting to confide in him. "I can't believe any more, Patrick. God doesn't answer my prayers. He's deaf where I'm concerned." The words came out in a rush. She'd never told anyone her doubts. Her religious beliefs were supposed to be unshakeable.

"Maybe you're the one who's not listening," Patrick said quietly.

"That's just priest doublespeak. You don't really know if anyone is listening to you, either."

"That's why they call it faith, Angie."

She sighed. "I've lost mine. That's why you haven't seen me at church. I can't pretend anymore. And don't tell my mother or sisters I said that, or I'll never hear the end of it."

"If you don't want to go into the church, come into the rectory. We'll have hot chocolate. I think I can drum up some whipped cream. You used to love that."

"I'm not that girl anymore. And you can't fix me, Patrick. I'm – I'm broken," she said, feeling a sense of overwhelming defeat.

"I don't believe that."

"It's true. What do all good Catholics do? They have big families and pass on the traditions of the family and the church. But not me. I can't seem to have a baby. The girl you thought could do anything can't do the simplest, most natural thing of all – bring a child into the world. I've tried in-vitro three times and nothing. Tonight Colin told me that he wouldn't do it again. He's forty years old. He wants us to plan a future with just him and me. But I can't find a way to give up on my dream of having my own child. I also can't imagine a future without Colin. I have no idea what we're going to do."

His eyes were gentle and sad. "I'm sorry, Angie."

"Yeah, me too." With tears pressing her eyelids, she turned to leave. She didn't want to break down in front of him.

"Come back," he called after her. "Don't worry about when or what time. Just come back when you're ready."

She paused on the sidewalk. "I won't ever be ready to come back to the church. Not unless I have a child with me."

"God likes a good challenge," he said

with a smile.

"Then he must love me."

"He does. You just don't know it."

* * *

"Is your name really John?" Liz sat back in her chair at the hotel bar. She felt pleasantly relaxed and a little buzzed after two and a half glasses of very expensive champagne. They'd spent the past hour conversing about nothing important – music, books, movies, and San Francisco. John was smart, funny, amazingly well read, and hot, a ridiculously good combination. There had to be something wrong with him. She was just not this lucky.

"Why wouldn't it be?" he countered.

"You don't look like a John, with your golden hair and your dark blue eyes. John is too plain, too average, and you are not either of those things."

"So what name would you like?"

"I don't know. Morgan or Drew or maybe one of those names that could be first or last, like Taylor or Tyler." She paused. "And besides the fact that John doesn't seem to fit you, every time I say your name, you seem a little surprised. So what's the story? Did you give me an alias? Are you running from the law?"

"Nothing that exciting. My first name is John, but my family mostly called me by my middle name, Eric, to differentiate between myself and my father, who was also named John."

"Then why didn't you introduce yourself as Eric?"

He ran his finger along the rim of his empty champagne glass, his gaze growing distant. "My dad is gone now, and everyone else who called me Eric is also gone. My mother died when I was a teenager. I don't have any siblings. It's just me." His voice was pragmatic, no hint of any emotion, but the tight line of his lips revealed his tension.

Now she better understood the hint of darkness that seemed to linger behind his smile. She didn't offer the usual, "I'm sorry." It wouldn't mean anything. His pain went soul deep. "Shall I call you Eric, or should I stick with John?"

He hesitated for a moment and then said, "Let's stick with John. I have my reasons," he added with a smile.

"You're good at turning the lights back on," she commented, taking another sip of champagne.

"What do you mean by that?"

"You get serious, then you shrug it off. Are you trying not to think about your dad?"

Surprise flashed through his eyes. "Maybe," he conceded. "You're very astute."

"I've always been a people watcher."

"Part of the job?"

"Yes. I like to be able to give someone what they need, even when they can't tell me they need it."

He met her gaze. "I like to do that, too. It feels good."

She smiled back at him. "That's why you brought me out for champagne. You didn't like my party of one, and you took pity on me."

"This is better, don't you think?"

"Absolutely."

"Good. Where is your family, Liz?"

She stiffened. She should have guessed that the inevitable personal questions would come up eventually. It was her fault. She'd started it by asking him about his name. If she'd just kept them focused on trivial topics, she might have been able to avoid this moment.

So tell the lie. It's no big deal. It's not like you haven't told it before. It's not like he's going to think you're not telling the truth.

"No one close by," she said vaguely.

"That's too bad."

She shrugged. "Since we're getting personal, what do you do for a living?"

"At the moment, I'm in between gigs, as they say."

"That's usually said about actors or musicians," she said pointedly. "Are you either one?"

"I always wanted to be a rock star, but

unfortunately, I couldn't sing." He paused as the waiter stopped by their table to ask if they wanted another drink.

Liz put a hand over her glass. "I won't be able to walk if I have any more."

"Well, we can't have that," he said, waving off the waiter. "It's early. I was thinking that we should keep the celebration going." A mischievous sparkle entered his eyes. "I know a great dance club south of Market."

She was tempted. She hadn't gone dancing in a couple of years. "I'm not dressed for it. I should be wearing a short dress with high heels and a pound of makeup."

"Who cares? We'll never see those people again."

"If they even let us in."

"Oh, we'll get in," he said confidently.

"You don't take no for an answer, do you?" She wondered what it would be like to attack life without any fear of rejection.

Another shadow filled his eyes. "Not if I can help it. So what you do say?"

"It might be fun," she said, very tempted to keep their party going. "You're not going to put down some incredible dance moves, are you?"

"You won't know unless you come. I dare you to say yes."

She smiled at his words. "Nobody has dared me to do anything since I was twelve years old and played Truth or Dare in Marcy Bennett's attic during her birthday slumber party."

"Did you pick truth or dare?"

"Dare."

"Interesting."

"Why is that interesting?"

"The choice says a lot about you. You'd rather do something crazy than answer some truth about yourself."

"Yeah, and from where I sit, you're exactly the same," she said pointedly.

He tipped his head. "Okay, tell me about the dare. What did you have to do?"

"I had to go into her parents' room and steal her father's slippers from under the bed without anyone waking up."

"Did you succeed?"

"No. I tripped over the dog. He started barking. Marcy's mother screamed because she thought I was a burglar. Mr. Bennett jumped out of bed stark naked. At the time, it seemed to me that his penis was enormous. I had never seen a grown man fully erect. It scared the hell out of me. Pretty soon we were all screaming. And that was pretty much the end of the game and the end of the party."

John started laughing and couldn't seem to stop.

"It's not funny," she said, biting back a laugh. "I was never invited back to Marcy's house again." She drank the last of her champagne. "So I don't do dares anymore."

"Yes, you do. I dared you to come out for a drink with me, and you came," he reminded her.

"Okay, but you caught me at a weak moment. I've been wanting to make some changes in my life, and your invitation seemed like a good place to start over, or again, or whatever you want to call it."

"Why do you want to change your life?"

"Because I want more," she said simply. "I want what everyone else has."

He leaned forward, his eyes curious. "And what do they have, Liz?"

It would sound silly to say it out loud, but the alcohol she'd consumed was acting like a truth serum. "Excitement, passion, all that crazy mad-about-you stuff. I want to fall in love." She drew in a breath. "And now I've probably scared you, and you're thinking, God, I hope she doesn't expect me to give her all that. I just asked her out for a drink."

He laughed. "I wasn't thinking that. You're very honest, Liz. I like it."

"I haven't really been that honest," she said slowly. "But I should probably start."

"What do you lie about?"

"Different things."

"Lies to keep people from knowing the real you?"

"Pretty much."

"Why?"

"That is way too long a story for tonight." She sighed as he gave her an expectant look. "I'll tell you this much. I had a boyfriend for three years. Kyle. I wanted to make it work, but he dumped me."

"Sorry."

"The worst part is that I should have been the one to walk. I was just too afraid of being alone. I hated being the single one with all my married friends. I didn't like going to the movies by myself. It was a very stupid reason for staying in a relationship."

"The devil you know…"

"Exactly. Kyle was solid and stable, had a good job, with goals and plans and budgets."

"That sounds exciting," John said dryly.

"He was someone I thought I could count on, and I needed that."

"You couldn't count on him that much – he dumped you."

She made a face. "Thanks for the reminder."

"Your words, not mine. In my opinion, you might be better off. Now you're free to find the person who's right for you."

"Yeah, that's going to be real easy."

John gave her a grin that was quickly becoming addictive. She'd never felt so comfortable with a man. She'd never been so honest, and it wasn't just the champagne. She liked him. He was charming and sexy, smart and quick, and he got her, and that was a heady mix of appealing. She needed to get a grip. He'd be gone in the morning. Tonight was not the start of something. It was just a few hours of fun. She didn't even know if he was involved with anyone, although she really hoped not. She probably should have asked that question an hour ago. Instead, she asked another. "What about you, John? Have you ever been in love?"

He hesitated and then said, "Once."

"Care to expand?" she prodded.

"It's not that good a story. I think we should continue on with your birthday celebration. Hey, this could be your birthday resolution: a night of new experiences."

"You're determined to have me make a resolution, aren't you?"

"It seems like a good one to me."

It seemed like a good one to her, too. "I'll go to a club with you, but after that I'm going home."

"We'll see." He pulled out his wallet and put some money on the table.

"Let me pay for half," Liz said, reaching for her purse. Unfortunately, she knocked it off the seat and the contents spilled onto the floor. "Damn," she muttered. Maybe she should make a resolution to not be so clumsy in the future.

She slid out of the booth to collect the contents of her purse. John knelt down to help her, and she saw his fingers close around the envelope a second too late. "Give me that," she said quickly.

He stared down at the envelope in his hand and then looked at her in surprise. "You know someone in prison?"

She swallowed hard. "Could I have it, please?"

He flipped it over. *Happy Birthday* was written across the back flap. "It's a birthday card. You haven't opened it yet."

"I'm not going to open it." She snatched the card from his hand. "Look, we can either go dancing or I can go home, but what we aren't going to do is talk about this. So what's it going to be?"

* * *

After leaving the church, Angela felt too restless to go home. Maybe she should have stayed with Patrick, talked to him more about her problems, but what did a priest know about trying to have a baby or working out a compromise with a spouse? Not that there was any way to compromise on the issue. They either tried again or they didn't. She wished she had someone in her life she could talk to who would be on her side. But all of her supporters had tired of the topic.

Her sisters continually reminded her that there were worse things in life than not being able to have a baby.

You should be grateful, Angie. Things could be worse. You could have cancer. You could lose all your money. You could get hit by a car tomorrow. Be happy with what you have.

She did have a lot of good things in her life, but that didn't make it easier to face a future without a baby in it. Her sisters had children, families to love and nurture, to watch grow and develop.

She couldn't call her mother, either. Her mom would just tell her that she'd waited too long to get started.

If only you'd listened to me, you wouldn't be in this predicament, Angela. You wasted the best childbearing years building a career and you waited too long to get your priorities straight.

And her friends would just offer false platitudes.

It's good that it's just you and Colin. You'll have money to travel around the world if you want, buy a bigger house, stay up late and make love in the middle of the kitchen. Kids aren't everything.

No, there was really no one she could talk to – so she drove aimlessly for another ten minutes, circling the Embarcadero, a street that ran around the outside of the city with the bay on one side and the skyscrapers on the other. There were seafood restaurants and tourists still lingering by Fisherman's Wharf and Ghirardelli Square. The city was alive and happy. She tried to take it in, soak it up, and feel better.

She had to think in practical terms, to stop whining about what she didn't have and what Colin wouldn't give her. She had to explore the alternatives. She could try the in-vitro on her own, using donor sperm. But would Colin support that? And if he didn't, was having a baby worth losing her marriage?

She could investigate surrogacy; have another woman carry her eggs and Colin's sperm and hope for a better outcome. She wouldn't have the experience of being pregnant, but she would have a baby at the end of it. It would be expensive, but she'd give up her business to make it work, if she had to. There had to be a way to get what she wanted.

Patrick had reminded her that when she wanted something, she usually made it happen. She'd been mentally defeated for too long. It was no wonder Colin didn't want to go through it all again. Her depression had been hard on him, too. She needed to convince him she could handle whatever came their way, as long as they didn't give up. She just needed a plan.

Spotting a small convenience store, she decided to stop for coffee and think for a few minutes before she headed back to the apartment. She would need all of her persuasive skills to convince Colin that a child was still in their future.

She pulled up along the curb, grabbed her bag, and got out of the car. A moment later she heard footsteps behind her. She suddenly realized how empty and dark this part of the street was. Except for the store on the corner, all of the other shops were closed and some had bars over the windows. She'd been so lost in thought she hadn't even considered her surroundings. That was stupid. She'd lived in the city long enough to know better.

She quickened her pace, but the footsteps were bearing down on her. She could hear the sound of someone breathing heavily.

Then a hand grabbed her arm.

Maybe there were worse things than not having a baby.

Chapter Four

As her assailant tried to yank the bag from her shoulder, something inside Angela snapped. She'd been feeling like a victim for too long. She couldn't let one more thing be taken from her, so she fought back. The figure in the dark hooded sweatshirt and baggy jeans was not that big, she realized, but they were determined. So was she.

She grabbed her bag and shoved her attacker backward. The hood slipped off her assailant's head, and she stared in shock as a long, tangled ponytail fell out.

Her mugger wasn't a man, but a girl – a young teenage girl with big brown eyes and dirty blond hair.

As the girl turned to bolt, Angela grabbed her arm. "Hold on."

"Let me go. I'm sorry," the girl blurted out, her eyes round and scared. "I'm just hungry."

"So you decided to rob me? How old are you?"

"Eighteen."

There was no way this child was eighteen. "Try again," she ordered.

"Why do you care?"

"Because you just attacked me."

"I wasn't trying to hurt you. Please don't call the police. I'm really sorry, and I swear I won't do it again," she said, struggling to break free.

"I'm not going to let you just walk away. Where do you live?"

"Nowhere near here."

Angela didn't believe her for a second. "I need a better answer, or I will call the police." She paused. "You're just a child. What were you thinking?"

"It wasn't for me," the girl said. "My sister is sick and I need to buy her some cough medicine."

"Where is your sister?" Angela asked, glancing around.

"She's at home. I gotta go. I can't leave her alone for long."

As the girl tried to break free, Angela found herself hanging on. There was fear in the girl's eyes and she obviously needed some help. But why did she care about a kid who'd just tried to steal her purse?

"Let me go," the girl pleaded. "My little sister gets scared when she's alone."

"Why is she alone? Where are your parents?" she asked, unable to let the matter drop.

"They're – out."

"What's your name?"

"It doesn't matter."

"It does matter. You need help."

"No one wants to help us. They just

want to split us up. My sister needs me. I
have to protect her."

She was getting in over her head, but
she couldn't seem to stop herself. "Where's
your sister?"

The girl hesitated. "I can't tell you.
You'll call the cops."

"I won't call the police – not yet,
anyway," she amended. "But if your sister is
sick and she needs medicine, maybe I can
help."

"If you want to help, give me some
money."

"First I need to meet your sister." She
paused. "I have sisters, too, one younger,
one older. I'd do anything for them."

"You seem nice," the girl muttered, as if
she was afraid to believe it.

"Then let me help you," she said
impulsively, trying not to think too hard
about her offer. She could be getting herself
into a dangerous situation. The girl could be
working for someone. There might not even
be a sister.

"I don't know why you'd want to," the
girl said, but despite the fear in her eyes,
there was also an edge of hope to her words.

"What's your name?" she asked again.
"Laurel."

The name seemed too pretty and soft for
her boyishly dressed, desperate attacker, but
she could certainly understand why Laurel
might feel safer out on the streets if she

looked more like a boy.

"Okay, Laurel. Take me to your sister."

"I hope I'm not making a mistake," Laurel said worriedly.

Angela met her gaze. "Me, too."

* * *

Carole grew tense as the limo took her toward the streets of her youth. Potrero Hill was in the southern section of the city. On one side of the hill, the houses and apartment buildings were well kept, rented or owned by families and professionals, but on the south side of the hill were two large low-income housing projects.

Second thoughts ran through her mind about this impulsive trip, her instinct for self-preservation telling her to turn back while she still had the chance. But she couldn't quite bring herself to tell the driver to stop. Something was missing from her life, and maybe if she retraced her steps, if she went back to where it had all begun, it would become clear exactly what that something was.

Or maybe she'd just realize that nothing was missing – that she had it all, every last item on the wish list she'd made as a child. Then she could go home and go on with her life.

Thankfully, her mother had moved out of the projects and into a small apartment building about four blocks away. While the three-story building showed signs of wear and tear, the yard was well kept, and there were even a few flowers in the first-story window boxes that hid the metal bars protecting the windows.

The driver opened her door and she stepped out on the sidewalk, shivering in the cold. She probably should have stopped to get her coat before leaving the hotel.

"Is this the right place?" the driver asked doubtfully.

"It is." She'd never visited, but this was the address she'd sent the compulsory Christmas card to every year for the last ten years. "Wait here. I'll just be a few minutes."

The front door to the building was ajar. If there was a security system, it was broken. She glanced down the list of residents and saw her mother's name, Nora Dennis, next to 2B. She walked into the lobby and skipped the elevator in favor of the stairs. She might not have lived in this type of neighborhood for a long time, but she knew better than to take an elevator in an old building.

Once upstairs, she took a deep breath and knocked on her mother's door. For a moment, she thought no one was home, and an odd mix of disappointment and relief swept through her. Then the door opened.

Her mother stared at her in shock. "Oh,

my Lord," she muttered, putting a hand to her heart.

Carole squared her shoulders, trying not to feel shocked as well. But it was difficult. She hadn't seen her mom in more than a decade, and time had taken its toll. The woman standing before her was a shell of her former vibrant self. Her hair was still red, but it was streaked with gray, and while her mother had always been skinny, a product of her cigarette-smoking habit, she was now so thin her cheeks were hollow and the shadows under her eyes were very pronounced. She was only sixty-three years old, but she looked at least ten years older. Probably the alcohol, Carole thought cynically. The last time she'd seen her mother, Nora had been falling-down drunk.

"Hello, Mom," she said, finally finding her voice.

"I can't say I ever expected to see you here, Carly," Nora said, shaking her head in bemusement.

"I never expected to be here."

"Is something wrong – your children–"

"No, she said, cutting her off. "My kids are fine, and so is my husband."

"Then…"

"It's my birthday."

"I know what day it is. I was there when you were born. I would have sent a card, but after the last few came back, I figured it was pointless. You've made it pretty clear that you don't want anything to do with me." A bright pain filled Nora's eyes.

"Can you blame me? The last time I invited you to a birthday party, my thirtieth, you showed up drunk. You insulted Blake. You called my daughter by the wrong name and made her cry, and you humiliated me." The words flew out of her mouth, fueled by some of the whiskey she'd drunk in the limo.

"And you've waited ten years to tell me that?" her mother asked wearily. She stepped away from the door and walked back into the apartment.

Carole followed her inside, closing the door behind her.

As she glanced around the small living room, she was struck by how much it looked like the home she'd grown up in. The coffee table was the same one she'd colored on. During one of her craft periods, her aunt had crocheted the afghan that hung over the back of the couch. And the pictures on the table were all from her childhood. Some were school pictures, others taken with kids in the neighborhood, a few of her mom and aunt with some of their friends. They were all from another lifetime.

She moved across the room and picked up the photo of the scene that had flashed through her mind only hours earlier. It had been taken on her eighth birthday, the candles blazing, just before Alex had shoved

Peter into her cake. She put down the photo and turned around.

Her mother sat on the couch and reached for her cigarettes.

"I'd rather you didn't smoke," Carole said quickly. "I can barely breathe in here as it is."

Her mother reluctantly set down the pack. "Why don't you say your piece and then you can go."

She wanted to do exactly that, but now that she was here, she couldn't find the words.

"You look pretty, Carly," her mother said, a sad, wistful note in her voice. "That's a beautiful dress. And you're so tan. Have you been on vacation?"

"It's a spray tan."

"Well, you look good. Were you at a party?"

She nodded. "My party."

"It's over early."

"It's not over; I left."

"Why?" Nora tilted her head, giving her a questioning look. The familiar gesture reminded her of all the times her mother had tried to figure her out. But as close as they'd been, they'd also been very different.

She sat down on the edge of a chair and clasped her hands together. "I'm forty."

"It's hard to believe," her mother acknowledged.

She blew out a breath. "I have no idea

why I'm here."

"Maybe you missed me," her mother suggested.

That idea would have seemed unthinkable only a few hours ago, but now in her mother's presence, surrounded by her past, she felt the ache in her heart go deeper. "Maybe," she conceded.

"Well," her mother said, surprise in her eyes, "that's something." Her gaze narrowed. "What did he do?"

"Who?"

"Your husband. Blake hurt you, didn't he?"

She twisted her wedding ring around her finger. "Not physically. Blake would never hit me the way Daddy–"

"I wasn't suggesting he hit you," Nora interrupted. "Only that he hurt you."

"I saw him with a woman. There was something between them. She was really young and very confident."

"They usually are."

"She gave me a smirking, pitying smile, as if she had something up on me. It was disgusting."

"So he's cheating on you?"

"No. Maybe. I hope not. I don't know." The words tumbled out of her, and she got up and walked restlessly around the small room. "I shouldn't have come here."

"Why not run to one of your friends?"

"I wouldn't want to suggest to any of

my friends that Blake was cheating on me. That's the last thing I would say."

"No one gets to see anything you don't want them to see," her mother said cynically. "Don't you get tired of the pretense, Carly?"

"Don't call me that. My name is Carole."

"Not in this house. You'll always be Carly to me no matter how expensive a dress you're wearing, or how much you spend to highlight your hair or do your nails. Underneath it all, you're still the girl who dipped Oreos into milk and played hopscotch on the sidewalk and snuggled with me in bed on Sunday mornings."

"My childhood was not all Oreos and hopscotch," she retorted. "It was also worrying about whether or not we'd have money for food, or if dad would come home high or drunk and want to beat the crap out of you."

A flush covered her mother's cheeks. "I can't change what happened with your dad. I kicked him out as soon as I could manage on my own."

"I was ten by then."

"I know exactly how old you were," Nora said fiercely. "If I could have found the strength when you were born or when you were two or five, I would have gotten away from him, but I was young and stupid, and I made mistakes. But through it all, I loved you with every ounce of my being. I have a lot to feel bad about, but I know in my heart I gave you a lot of love. And for a long time, you loved me back."

Now she was the one feeling guilty.

"I don't think you came here just to yell at me," Nora added. "But I could be wrong. You've changed a lot over the years. Maybe you just needed to get rid of the hatred in your heart. Is that it?"

"No, that's not it. I'm just – confused. And I haven't changed all that much. I just grew up, that's all," she said defensively.

"You didn't just grow up, you grew cold."

How could a woman she hadn't seen in more than a decade still know her better than anyone else?

Nora stood up. "I wish I could stay and talk to you. Lord knows I have a lot I'd like to say, questions to ask. I want to know about my grandbabies. I want to know about you, but I have to go to work, Carly."

"It's almost ten o'clock. The diner isn't open this late."

"I'm also helping your Aunt Eileen with her cleaning service. She does the law building on Evans Street at night."

"You're working two jobs? But I send you money." It was the one thing she did to allay some of the guilt she felt over their broken relationship.

"And I have it all in a bank account

with your children's names on it. They'll get
it back when I die."

"What are you talking about? That
money is for you. My kids have what they
need."

"And I don't *need* your money. I never
wanted your charity, Carly. I wanted you in
my life. You're my daughter."

"I wanted you in my life, too, but the
last time I tried, you were drunk. You made
an ass of yourself, and Blake told me he
didn't want you back."

"It wasn't my finest moment," Nora
conceded. "I admit that. You might not
believe it, but I drank so much that night
because I was nervous. It was the first time
you'd invited me to your fancy house with
your rich friends, and I didn't think I was
going to fit in. I wasn't sure how to act, but I
went too far."

"All you had to do was be sober. That
wasn't a lot to ask."

Her mother shook her head, bitterness
in her eyes. "That's not all you wanted me to
be, Carly. You wanted me to be the mother
you wished you had, the one you could be
proud of, and I was never going to be that,
sober or otherwise. You think I don't know
why you were so eager to grow up and get
out from under me?"

Carole felt another twinge of guilt. "I
just wanted a better life."

"Well, you got what you wanted." Nora

grabbed her car keys and bag and headed toward the door.

She followed her mother into the hall, waiting as she locked the doors, wishing she knew what to say, because her mother was about to take off, and she felt more unsettled now than she had been before she arrived. In fact, she didn't feel forty anymore; she felt about fifteen. And that was a really weird feeling. She was still searching for words when they went down the stairs and out to the street.

Her mother paused, giving the limo a long glance. "That's nice."

"Blake rented it for my birthday. Let me give you a ride to work."

"I've got my car."

"Mom, wait," she said impulsively as her mother turned to leave.

"What?"

"I want to talk to you some more. We need to continue this conversation."

Surprise flashed in her mom's eyes. "Really?"

"Yes. I didn't realize how much unfinished business I had until I got here. What time do you get off?"

"Around one."

That was almost three hours away. The smart thing to do would be to go home and come back in the morning, but she had the strange sense that whatever needed to be said needed to be said tonight. "I'll drop you off at work, and then pick you up at one," she said impulsively.

Nora gave her a doubtful look. "What are you going to do in the meantime?"

"I don't know. I'll figure something out."

"What about your husband?"

"He probably hasn't even noticed I'm gone," she lied.

"I doubt that."

"It doesn't matter. I could use some time away from Blake. And the kids are both sleeping at friend's houses. Blake and I were going to stay at the Remington Hotel. He rented a suite for my birthday."

"Then that's where you should be."

"I can't be with him tonight."

"He won't like it."

"I'm not afraid of him."

"But you've let him run your life."

She couldn't deny that there was some truth in her mother's words. "Maybe, but that was my choice. Now, it's my choice to spend some time with you. So how about that ride?"

"Okay," her mother said finally.

She opened the door. "After you."

Chapter Five

A few minutes later Carole dropped her mother off at the law offices. As she debated her options, her gaze settled on the familiar neon sign for Murphy's Tavern. She had some time to kill. If she was going to take a trip down memory lane, she might as well see all the old sights.

"I'm going to get a drink," she told the driver. "I'll give you a call when I'm ready to leave." She hurried down the street, wishing again she had a coat, but in many ways the cold air was invigorating. She felt more alive than she had in a long time.

Murphy's Bar had been a landmark on the hill for at least fifty years. It was a working-class neighborhood bar with beer, burgers, sports and good friends. She'd had her first illegal drink at Murphy's at seventeen, but while her fake ID had worked on the part-time bartender, the owner, Donald Murphy, had thrown her out about five minutes later.

She hadn't really been surprised. Donald Murphy knew all the kids in town. He had six children of his own, and he was a familiar figure on the soccer and baseball fields where he coached or umpired games.

He'd been a mentor and father figure for her and a lot of her friends.

As she walked inside the bar, she found herself hoping he'd be there. She could use a dose of his Irish charm, his practical, down-to-earth, no-nonsense wisdom. But as she entered Murphy's, the man behind the bar had jet-black hair and a very familiar set of shoulders. As her gaze met his amazing light blue eyes, her entire world spun around.

Recognition flashed in his gaze, a mix of surprise, anger, welcome and wariness. "Carly?"

His deep voice took her back in time. He'd said her name many, many times in her childhood, adolescence, and young-adult years – sometimes with anger, sometimes with love, sometimes with passion…

She struggled to breathe, to find her voice, to say something. But what?

Alex had been so many things to her – the annoying boy across the hall who had ruined her birthday cake, the attractive teen with whom she'd shared her first real kiss, the guy who'd helped her move her meager belongings into her dorm room, and finally, the man who'd asked her to marry him.

Her legs felt weak, and she slid onto the nearby bar stool with relief. She hadn't seen Alex since she'd turned down his proposal eighteen years ago. She'd been twenty-two and had her sights set on an up-and-coming young lawyer in the law firm where she worked in downtown San Francisco. She hadn't known what would happen then with Blake, but she'd been fairly sure that if she said yes to Alex, she would never get off the hill.

Alex moved down the bar. He'd grown up, filled out, his hair graying at the temples, his shoulders broader than she remembered, his jaw stubborn, his lips still sexy. She blew out a breath. It was amazing that she could have such a strong reaction to a man she hadn't seen in almost two decades, but Alex had always had a way with the women. It was those Black Irish looks. They were a killer. Her gaze moved to his hand. He didn't wear a ring, but that didn't necessarily mean that he wasn't married.

"What can I get you?" he asked, his tone even, his gaze guarded.

He was talking to her like any other customer, which was just – wrong.

Carly?" he asked again, an edge to his voice now. "I don't have all day."

She drew in a breath. "Sorry. I'll have a glass of beer. Whatever you have on tap."

"Beer? Seriously?" he asked cynically. "Haven't you moved on to more sophisticated drinks?"

"Beer is fine," she said, meeting the challenge in his gaze. "Apparently, the years between had not improved his opinion of her.

He poured a beer and set it down in

front of her. Then he moved down the counter to help another customer.

She was grateful for the momentary reprieve. She sipped her beer and glanced around the room. There was a decent crowd. Most of the tables were full, and there was a crowd gathered around the pool table in the back. It was a mix of young and old, all casually dressed. She looked very out of place in her evening gown, but then, she probably would have felt out of place in her designer jeans, too. She'd outgrown this bar a long time ago.

A young woman moved behind the bar, wearing black pants and a white top. "Sorry that took so long," she told Alex.

"No problem," he said.

As the woman started to attend to the customers at the bar, Alex walked back to her.

"Nice dress, Carly."

"I'd say thank you if your tone wasn't so sarcastic," she replied.

He met her gaze. "What did you expect?"

"Nothing. I didn't even know you would be here."

Disbelief shadowed his eyes. "Then what are you doing here?"

"Just getting a drink."

"Here? Out of all the bars in this city, you decided to have a drink here?"

"It was an impulsive decision." She

paused. "How can you still be mad at me?"

"I'm not angry. I haven't thought of you in years," he said. "And I'm sure the same is true for you. Once you left, you never looked back, did you?"

She met the challenge in his gaze. "I tried not to."

"There you go." He leaned against the counter behind him and crossed his arms. "So what are you doing here?"

"I wanted to see my mom," she said, not sure that was really the reason, but it was the only one she could voice.

"I didn't think you two spoke any more."

"We haven't in a long time. We had a big blowout fight a while back."

He nodded. "She told me."

"You talk to my mom?" It was a stupid question. Of course he did. He worked at Murphy's. "I should have realized. This is a bar after all."

"Not here," he said quickly. "Nora doesn't drink any more. I usually catch up with her at the diner."

"She gave up drinking?" she asked doubtfully.

"Right after that fight the two of you had." He gave her a hard look. "She felt really bad about ruining your birthday party."

"She should have felt bad. You have no idea how humiliating her behavior was."

"Not just for you – for her, too." He paused, then added, "She always loved you, Carly, even when she screwed up."

"Which was a lot."

"Maybe. But it wasn't just her mistakes that bothered you – it was who she was. She wasn't enough for you. No one in this neighborhood was good enough for you, including me. So what the hell are you doing here?"

She drew in a quick breath at the unexpected attack. "It's my birthday," she blurted out. "My fortieth birthday."

"I know how old you are, and what day it is, but you still haven't answered my question."

"I don't really know," she said with a sigh. "Birthdays have always been a disaster for me, and I guess this one won't be any different."

"You had some good parties when I knew you."

"Really? Like the one where you smashed my cake?"

He raised an eyebrow. "Excuse me?"

"On my eighth birthday. You shoved Peter, and he fell into the cake and set his hair on fire."

Alex's lips turned up in a reluctant smile, reminding her of her best friend from childhood, the one who used to like her.

"I do remember that," he said. "You were so pissed and afraid you weren't going to get your wish. You never told me if you did." He gave her a quizzical look.

"Does it matter?" She picked up her beer and took a sip.

"So what happened tonight? Why aren't you with your husband and your kids celebrating your birthday?"

"I was with them for a while."

"And?"

"My kids left. They had other things to do."

"More important than their mother's birthday?"

She didn't like his question. More important, she didn't like the perceptive gleam in his eyes. Alex had always been able to read her a little too well, and she didn't need him knowing that her life was not as perfect as she'd planned. She never should have come back here. But now she couldn't leave. She'd promised her mom she would pick her up in a few hours. Not that she had to stay in the bar. She could drive around, even go home and change clothes, then come back. It wasn't that far. Going home, however, might involve Blake and explanations, and she couldn't handle any of that right now, although, Blake was probably still at the party entertaining his friends.

"What's going on with you?" Alex asked, tilting his head thoughtfully.

"I guess this birthday hit me harder than

I thought it would."

"Forty is scary. Thank God I'm not there yet."

"You're a month behind me."

"But not there yet. I'm still young."

"Thanks," she said dryly.

"You know what I always admired about you, Carly?"

"I didn't think there was much you admired about me."

"You were always sure of what you wanted. You had a to-do list, a plan for the future. And you went after your goals with relentless determination."

"You hated that about me," she reminded him.

He tipped his head. "Only because your plans were taking you away from me, but I still admired your fire, your drive. Now there's doubt in your eyes, as if you're not sure what you're going to do five minutes from now, much less five years."

"I'm *not* sure." She took another long draught of beer and then said candidly, "I thought I'd be happier, Alex."

"I'm surprised you'd admit your life isn't perfect."

"I'm surprised, too, but there it is."

"Well, I can't say I'm not a little happy to hear that, considering you dumped me for a better life."

"I wasn't right for you, Alex. We didn't want the same things."

"I just wanted you. You were the one who made things complicated."

"That's probably true. I've never done anything the easy way."

"So did something happen tonight specifically?" he asked.

She hesitated. She never talked about her private life with anyone, not even her friends, but here was a guy who'd seen her at her worst. What did she really have to lose by telling the truth? He wasn't part of her world, and after tonight, it would no doubt be another decade before she saw him again.

"I think my husband is having an affair." The words flew out of her mouth. "Or he's considering it."

"That sucks."

"Yes, it does, and you should have seen the woman he was flirting with. She was so young; it was disgusting."

"What are you going to do?"

"What can I do? I married him. I have children with him. Not that my kids would miss Blake. He hasn't been around much in the last few years." She paused, another truth itching to get out. "I'm not much better, Alex. I've been so busy being the perfect wife that I haven't always been the best mother. I always put Blake first and the kids second. I wanted them to have the childhood I didn't have, the money, the big house, the vacations and clothes. But now I feel like we're strangers. My kids are teenagers, and they left my birthday party before I cut the cake. But how can I blame them for taking off when I did the same thing to them so many times? When I blew out the candles tonight, I looked around the room and realized there wasn't anyone there who knew me – the real me – and it rattled me."

"You got rid of the real you when you got married. You were itching to ditch your life the first second you could. I saw the restlessness long before you actually left me."

She sipped her beer, feeling a little overwhelmed by the intensity in his look. He was making her feel things she'd thought were long dead. She needed to change the subject. "What about you, Alex? Are you married?"

"I'm divorced."

"I'm sorry."

"But not surprised. What did you say before? Oh, I know – I wasn't marriage material."

She sighed. "Do you really want to go back there, Alex? Rehash our past?"

He shrugged. "You tell me. You're the one who walked into my bar."

"Your bar?" she echoed. "What happened to Donald Murphy?"

"He retired. He sold me the bar five years ago."

Staring into his proud eyes, she realized Alex had gotten what he always wanted, the opportunity to be his own boss. And she *was* a little surprised. Alex had had dreams but never any concrete plan for how to make his dreams happen. She'd obviously sold him a little short. "That's great. You always loved this place."

"I do love it," he said, glancing around the room with an approving eye. "It's home – literally. I took the apartment upstairs after the divorce."

"No kids?"

A shadow flashed through his eyes. "No. I wanted some, but it was never the right time, and then it was too late." He paused. "I can't believe you have teenagers."

"I got pregnant right away. Blake wanted a family, and so did I, and we didn't see any reason to wait. He had as many plans as I did, and he still does. "He's going to run for the state senate next year."

"Your mother told me your husband's ambition is even bigger than yours."

"I can't believe you and my mother talk about me."

"Not that often, but on occasion. Talking to me about you, about the old times, makes the distance between you hurt a little less."

"I never wanted to hurt her," she said with a sigh.

"That's why you didn't talk to her for ten years?"

"I've sent her cards. But she screwed up big time, and Blake really didn't want her to be around us or the kids."

"And it's his call?" Alex challenged. "I thought you had a spine to go with all that ambition. Or did you give that up, too, when you got married?"

"You don't know me at all anymore." She slid off her stool. "I should go."

"Getting a little too hot in here?"

"There's no point to this conversation."

"Does there have to be a point? We're just catching up."

"I suppose."

"And I don't think you're ready to go."

"Well, I did tell my mother I'd pick her up from work, so I have some time to kill, but I don't have to do it here."

"Why don't you come upstairs?"

A tingle shot down her spine. He wasn't suggesting a hook-up, was he? She should be angry, furious, but the emotion running through her felt more like excitement.

"We can talk," Alex added, his gaze narrowing. "You didn't think…"

"No, of course not," she said quickly. "I'm married."

"Right. Upstairs might not be a good idea. In fact, I have a better one."

"What's that?"

"It will be a surprise."

She gave him a doubtful look. "I don't like surprises."

"I know. You like to plan and control every moment of your life, but you're taking a trip down memory lane, and I don't want you to miss any of the important spots."

"What are you talking about?"

"You'll see." He turned to the other bartender. "I'll be back in a while." As the woman nodded, he moved through the door behind the bar and returned a moment later with a big coat. "You're going to need this."

"This is not a good idea," she said as she took the coat.

He grinned. "It won't be the first bad idea I've had, especially where you're concerned."

"You always could talk me into things."

"Only when you secretly wanted to do them," he said, once again reminding her of just how well he knew her. Almost twenty years had passed, but she felt like a young girl again… and hell, maybe that was worth something. Why not have a reckless night? She was forty. Tomorrow and reality would come soon enough.

* * *

Following her would-be mugger home was not the smartest idea Angela had ever had, but she felt a force propelling her forward that seemed impossible to resist.

The apartment building was only a block away from the convenience store and had obviously seen better days. Everything was old. The hallways smelled of cigarette smoke and a mix of other food smells. Through the thin walls, she could hear a couple yelling at each other.

Laurel stopped in front of a door on the second floor and unlocked the two locks. She led the way inside, calling for her sister. "Kimmie, I'm back."

A small girl of about six or seven came running around the couch with a ragged stuffed bear in her arms. She barreled into Laurel as she shot Angela a suspicious look. "Who's she?" she asked.

"I'm Angela," she replied.

She looked around the small, dark, dirty apartment, even more appalled at the living conditions. There were no lights on, just a couple of candles casting big shadows on walls of peeling paint. The blinds at the windows were broken. A queen-sized bed in one corner was unmade, and the couch was messy with pillows and blankets. "Where is your mother?" she asked.

"She's been gone a long time," Kimmie announced.

Laurel glared at her sister, then looked back at Angela. "Not that long, and she'll be back. She always comes back eventually."

"Is the electricity off?"

"We like candles," Laurel said

defensively.

"Do you have heat?"

"It's not that cold. We have blankets. We just need a little money for food and some cough medicine," Laurel added as Kimmie gave a congested cough. "We'll pay you back."

"How on earth would you do that?"

"I'll find a way," Laurel said, lifting her chin.

"I need to call someone to help you."

"You can't," Laurel said quickly. "They'll split us up, and Kimmie needs me."

Angela stared at the two little girls clinging together and couldn't help but be reminded of herself and her sisters. But they had grown up in a loving family, a beautiful home. They'd had so much more than this. It was criminal the way the girls were living.

"My aunt said she'd come on Sunday," Laurel put in. "We'll be okay until then if you can give us a few dollars."

She didn't know if there was an aunt, but she seriously doubted it. Laurel would do anything to keep her and her sister together. Angela debated her options. This wasn't her problem. She could call the cops and hand the girls off and know they'd be taken care of, maybe not the way they wanted, but they would be safe and fed and provided with care. That was the most important thing.

"Please," Laurel said, obviously sensing

she was losing the battle. "Don't turn us in."

"You can't live here alone, honey."

"We've been alone before, and we were fine."

"You're not fine. You're hungry, and Kimmie is sick."

"You don't know what it's like in the homes they send us to. It's horrible."

Kimmie started to cry, and Angela wasn't sure if it was because she knew what was coming or she was just picking up on her sister's fear. Her sobs were mixed with coughs and big sniffs.

"Okay, stop crying," she said. "You're going to make yourself feel worse."

"I don't want to leave Laurel. She takes care of me," Kimmie whined. "She holds my hand when it's dark, and it's really dark outside now."

It was dark. It was very late. She'd been gone for hours, driving around feeling sorry for herself.

Well, she wanted to be a mother, and right now there were two children in front of her who needed some nurturing. "I won't call anyone tonight," she said, making an impulsive decision that she hoped she wouldn't regret. "I'll wait until the morning, but you two are coming home with me. I can't leave you here alone, and you need food. You can come to my house. We'll leave your mother a note and tell her where you are in case she comes back."

The girls were too desperate to ask any questions, even though they probably should have. She was a stranger, but obviously in their world they had to take a chance on who to trust, and right now they were trusting her.

She jotted down her name and phone number and a quick note of explanation while Laurel grabbed some clothes for her and Kimmie.

When they left the apartment, Angela had no idea if she was doing the right thing, but she was doing something, taking action, and it felt good. She just hoped Colin would agree.

Chapter Six

"Are you crazy?" Colin asked as Angela finished telling him that Laurel and Kimmie were going to stay with them for the night. "You can't just take someone else's kids and bring them home."

"I'll explain more in a minute." She glanced down at the girls, who were practically hiding behind her. Colin's anger had obviously scared them. "The girls are hungry. I hope there are leftovers." She was more than a little thankful that the party had ended before she got back. It was going to be difficult enough to explain what she'd done to Colin.

"Of course. Your mother makes enough food to feed an army," he replied, running a hand through his hair in frustration.

"Let's get some dinner, girls," she said, heading toward the kitchen. "My mom made three kinds of lasagna. I hope you like Italian."

"What's lasagna?" Kimmie asked.

"It's like spaghetti with big flat noodles," Angela answered. "You can wash your hands, and I'll heat up some pasta for you."

Laurel pulled a kitchen chair over to the

sink for Kimmie to stand on and then turned on the water.

Angela quickly pulled out salad, lasagna and bread, acutely aware of Colin standing in the doorway. "As soon as I get them settled, I'll talk to you," she told him.

He gave a helpless shake of his head and then left the room.

She made up two plates of food and set them on the table while the girls took a seat.

"Is this for us?" Kimmie asked in wonder.

"Eat as much as you like," Angela told them.

The girls dove in before she had finished speaking. It was clear they'd been hungry for a while.

"You don't have to rush," she added. "There's more where that came from." She watched them for another minute and then returned to the living room.

Colin had a trash bag in one hand and was collecting used paper plates and cups, a reminder of the birthday party she'd run out on.

"Where should I start?" she asked, twisting her hands together.

He set down the trash bag and planted his hands on his hips. "Why don't you start with where you've been for the last three hours?"

"I drove around for a while. I never meant to be gone so long, but I needed to think."

"We were worried about you. Your mother and sisters were very upset."

"I'll apologize to them tomorrow."

She sat on the sofa and drew in a breath. Colin took a seat on the ottoman in front of his favorite armchair. He stared at her for a long moment. "I feel like I don't even know you anymore," he murmured.

She was feeling a little that way herself. She'd been restless for months, but her birthday had brought everything to the boiling point.

"Tell me again what happened," he said. "You drive around and then stumble upon two homeless girls and decide to bring them home?"

She hadn't told him that Laurel had attempted to mug her, something she intended to leave out of her story for the time being. "They need help. Their mom is away and there's no electricity at their apartment."

"Then you should have called the police."

"Laurel said when the police come, they always split them up. Kimmie is scared and has a cold and needs to be with her sister."

"Angie, this is not our problem."

"I know that, but I couldn't look the other way, Colin. I saw two young girls who needed someone to help them. So I did."

"You should have taken them to the

police station."

"I thought about it, but it's late, and I didn't think one more night would make a difference."

"What if their mother comes home and finds them gone?"

"I considered that. I left a note with our phone number."

"Oh, that's great. The mother could be a crazy person, a drug addict. She could be a criminal and now she has our phone number."

"I didn't know what else to do. Laurel said she thought her mother would be back by Sunday, or that her aunt would come."

He shook his head. "Angie, these kids need professional support. I know you want to be a mother, but this is ridiculous. You can't just grab two kids and bring them home. You've lost your mind. I'm calling the police." He stood up.

"Wait. Just let them stay until the morning, Colin. I made them a promise, and I want to keep it. What are a few hours? It's not like we don't have the room."

His gaze narrowed. "Will you really call tomorrow? Or will you have another reason for keeping them just a little longer?"

"I just want to be sure they're taken care of. I need to think about the best thing to do."

"You need to think about a lot of things, like why you blew off your own birthday party, why you can't be happy in a marriage with just the two of us, and why you think you can somehow take two kids off the street and become an instant mother."

"It's been a bad night," she said quietly, realizing that his frustration had to do with more than just Laurel and Kimmie's arrival. "I'm sorry that I ran out on the party. And while I want to say I could be happy in a marriage without children, I don't think I can. I love you, Colin. It's not that you're not enough – it's that *I'm* not enough. Something is missing inside of me. I ache. And I don't think that feeling is going to go away. I need to be a mother."

He sat back down on the ottoman, his eyes bleak. "I don't know what to say. I understand, but I can't give you a miracle, and that's what it might take for you to have a baby. I also can't keep having this conversation with you. I can't face the disappointment that seems inevitable every time we try to make a baby. Do you know that in the last three years, I actually knew exactly when your period was going to come? Do you know that I dreaded coming home those days, knowing that I'd find you in tears? Every single month, you cried."

"I'm sorry. It was hard to hold in the pain."

"And it was hard for me to see it, to know that I couldn't give you what you wanted. Now you want to start again. And all the schedules, treatments and clinical dissection of our reproductive challenges are too much for me. I want to talk about other things. I want to have a life that's happy and just not so damn stressful. I love you, too, Angela, but I don't know where we go from here."

Her heart sank with his words. "I don't want to lose you, Colin."

"Maybe you do."

She was shocked by his stark response and immediately shook her head. "No, I don't. How can you say that?"

"Another man might be able to give you a baby."

"It's more my problem than yours."

"No, it's both of us, but with one of us out of the equation…"

A wave of nausea ran through her. "Colin, I don't want another man."

"Even if it meant you could have a baby?"

"I want you and a baby. Why is that so wrong? It's what everyone else has."

"It's not wrong. It's just what it is."

She stared back at him, suddenly realizing that the scenario he'd suggested a few minutes earlier worked the other way, too. "Maybe you want another woman."

"I don't. I married you, Angie, for better or worse, but I can't make the impossible happen. And even if I agreed to try another fertility treatment, there's no guarantee of a better outcome. Then what? Another try and another? When will it be enough?"

"I don't know, but I'm thirty-five, and right now I have a little window of time to make something happen." She drew in a deep breath, feeling like they were going around in circles, which was what they'd been doing the last few years. She understood Colin's weariness. She felt it, too. She just wasn't ready to admit defeat. "We can talk about this tomorrow. I want to get the girls settled in for the night."

"You have to call the police in the morning, Angie."

"I know. But tonight I'm going to make sure the girls are fed and washed and have a nice bed to sleep in. It's not a lot to offer them, but it's something."

"You have a big heart." He paused. "You would make an incredible mother." He got up and walked over to her, pulling her to her feet. He kissed her tenderly on the mouth. "I do love you. No matter what happens, never doubt that."

Her eyes blurred with tears. Even when Colin was angry, he was always kind. He would make a great father. "Why does this have to be so hard?" she murmured.

"I don't know. But what I do know is that we can't go on like this." His eyes darkened. "Tomorrow, we're both going to have to make some hard decisions."

* * *

Liz didn't want the night to end. She didn't know if John was crazy, or she was, but ever since she'd met him on the roof of the hospital, she'd become a different person – a person she was starting to like, a person who couldn't seem to stop smiling. After leaving the Remington Hotel, they'd gone to a trendy new club in a converted old brick building. While the bouncer had looked disparagingly at her less than exciting outfit, John had said something to him, and the next minute they'd been allowed inside.

Since then they'd been dancing to a D.J. for over an hour. She was sweating and tired but also feeling more alive than she had in a long time.

John grinned as he grabbed her hand and spun her around for the thousandth time. The dance floor was packed, but he didn't seem to care. He was the kind of man used to owning his space. She envied his confidence, his ability to be the center of attention and not give a damn what anyone around them was thinking.

She'd worried too hard and for far too long about other people's opinions. She needed to start living her life and not the life others thought she should have. Sometime between lighting the candle on her cupcake and making a wish, her entire world had shifted – in a good way.

As the music ended and couples headed back to the bar area, John leaned in and said in her ear, "Ready to go?"

She wasn't nearly ready, but the man had already spent several hours with her. He'd made her birthday special, and it was time to let him go. "Yes," she said, then followed him to the door.

The street was quiet after the loud chaos of the club. The cold air turned the beads of sweat on her forehead and arms into goose bumps.

"We need a cab," John said, putting his arm around her shoulders. "You're cold."

"I'm fine. It feels good."

"You're too nice, Liz."

She frowned. "When a man calls you *nice*, it's usually the kiss of death."

He laughed. "I didn't mean it that way."

"Sure, whatever." She looked down the street, searching for a taxi.

"Hey, seriously." John waited for her to look at him. "You're very cool, Liz."

"Well, *cool* sounds better than *nice*," she conceded. "You're not bad yourself."

He stared back at her, the humor in his gaze replaced by something more serious. Her breath caught in her throat, the tension building between them. And then a cab pulled up at the curb and a couple jumped out.

"We should grab this," John said.

Disappointment swept through her. For

a minute there, she'd thought he wanted to kiss her. He held the door open for her, and she slipped into the back seat. It was almost midnight, and her fairytale was about to end.

John gave the driver an address she wasn't familiar with, and her heart sped up again. Was he assuming she'd go home with him?

He settled back in his seat and said, "I'm hungry. There's an all night cafe that makes the most amazing chili cheese fries."

"The last thing I need to eat is chili cheese fries at midnight."

"This is the night for doing everything you wouldn't ordinarily do. Remember your birthday resolution?"

"I don't think that was my resolution," she protested. Not that it was a bad one. What she'd been doing hadn't been working. Why not mix things up? "All right, chili cheese fries it is. Tomorrow I'll work out."

A few minutes later, the cab pulled up outside a coffee shop in a part of the city called Potrero Hill.

"I've never been in this neighborhood," she said as she stepped out of the cab.

"I used to live here," John replied. "On one of the few blocks that escapes the fog. It was amazing to sit in the sun watching the fog cover the city like a thick blanket."

She looked out at the view from the hill. There was no fog tonight, just an array of city lights and twinkling stars that once again gave her the crazy feeling that tonight, anything was possible.

"Come on," John said, grabbing her hand. "You can stargaze later."

As they walked down the street toward the restaurant, Liz paused. "Hey, isn't that the woman from the birthday party?" she asked, as a tall, thin blonde in an evening dress walked out of a bar across the street. She had a big coat on over her turquoise dress but it was definitely the same woman.

"I think so," John said.

"That's not her husband," she commented, noting the man in the jeans and leather jacket following her out of the bar.

"Certainly doesn't look like the guy who toasted her."

"She was having a huge birthday party at a downtown hotel. I wonder how she got from there to here," Liz mused.

The couple walked down the street, fading into the shadows on the opposite corner.

"It's a mystery," John said as he opened the door to the coffee shop. "Maybe like you, her birthday took an unexpected turn."

"It seems to be the night for that," she said, following him inside.

The coffee shop wasn't as empty as she would have expected so late in the evening. Almost all the booths were full. They settled at a corner booth and ordered coffee and chili cheese fries, as well as a salad to make her feel better about balancing out the carbs.

"So it's time," John proclaimed.

She raised an eyebrow as a shiver ran down her spine. "For what?"

"A little talking."

"Haven't we been doing that all night?"

"The birthday card in your purse."

She felt like he'd just stabbed her in the gut. "I told you, we aren't talking about that."

"This is the night of doing what you don't normally do."

"I'm not going that far."

"Who's the card from?"

"It's not important," she said fiercely, fighting the urge to answer his question. But there was something about John that made him a very hard man to say no to.

"It has to be important. You're carrying the card around in your bag."

"I just haven't had a chance to get rid of it." She sighed in the face of his unrelenting stare. "Do you ever let anything go?"

"I used to, but I've recently learned that putting things off until tomorrow isn't a very good idea. Sometimes tomorrow doesn't come."

"You're talking about your dad."

He shrugged. "It's your call, but I can't believe that you're holding on to a card that means nothing to you."

She hesitated another second and then

gave in. "It's from my father."

"How long has he been in prison?"

"Almost ten years. I was nineteen when he was arrested, twenty when he went to jail. I was in college at the time – premed. My plan was to be a doctor. But after he was arrested, my parents' assets were frozen, and there was no money for my education. I dropped out for a while, went to work, saved my money, and eventually got into nursing school with some help from my grandmother."

"What did your father do?"

"He was a con man, a white-collar investor. He ripped off a lot of people including our family and friends. He lied, cheated and hurt everyone I loved," she said, the words rushing out now that she'd set them free. "I never imagined that he could be guilty, but as the truth came out it was clear that he'd been cheating people for years."

"I'm sorry," John said gently.

"It's not your fault. It's his." She took a breath. "He wants me to forgive him, and maybe if it were just for the fraud, I could, but he's the reason my mother took a bottle of sleeping pills a year later and never woke up."

John stiffened, his eyes filling with compassion. "Oh, my God. Liz. I had no idea. You don't have to talk about this."

"You started it. Now I seem to be

compelled to finish." She hadn't talked about any of this with anyone in a very long time. Not even Kyle had ever heard more than the bare details, and he'd never been interested enough to press for more information. But in retrospect Kyle was fairly self-absorbed and if it hadn't had to do with him, he didn't care that much. John, however, seemed to want to know more. And for some odd reason, she wanted to tell him. "It was on her wedding anniversary," she continued. "My mother couldn't stand the shame he'd brought upon them or the rumors suggesting that she'd known what he was doing, perhaps even helped him."

John nodded. "That must have been rough."

"It was horrible. Now it seems almost commonplace. In recent years, more swindlers have been revealed with crimes of even bigger proportion, but ten years ago my dad's scam was somewhat legendary. For weeks reporters camped outside our house. They'd follow my mother when she went to the supermarket. Sometimes they'd follow me, and I knew nothing. He was just my dad. I had no idea he was a con man." She paused. "He's sorry now, and he wants a second chance, but my mother didn't get one. Why should he?"

He gave her a thoughtful look. "Are you angry with your mother, too?"

She wished she could say no, but there

was an anger inside her that had never gone away. "A little. I don't understand why she did it."

"She wanted to escape the pain."

"What about my pain? I needed her to fight, not to give up. Suicide is cowardly."

"Maybe she wasn't as strong as you are."

"Well, I'm stronger now because I had to keep going. I couldn't check out the way she did." She blew out a breath. "I can't believe I just said all that out loud. It seems wrong to be mad at her. She was obviously hurting. I should have more compassion. But I don't understand why she couldn't fight for me, if not for herself. I needed her. Some days I didn't know how I was going to get up in the morning. But she obviously wasn't thinking about me when she took those pills."

"I'm sorry, Liz. You've had a rough time."

"Because of their choices," she said. "Not because of fate or some disease. That's what makes it so hard. None of it had to happen, the crime, the suicide. But it did." She paused, feeling a little lighter for having gotten the words out. "I never told anyone what I just told you."

"Not even Kyle?"

"No. He wasn't that interested. Or maybe he sensed a story that he didn't want to hear."

"He sounds like a loser."

"Not really, but he wasn't the right guy. So, are you sorry you asked about my birthday card?"

"Actually, I'm not."

"I know I feel a little too sorry for myself. Other people have it just as bad or even worse. You had to watch your father suffer through a long illness. That wasn't easy."

"No, it was very difficult. He fought as hard as he could for as long as he could. He was an amazing man. Stronger than I'll ever be. I could never live up to him."

"I'm surprised you would say that. You have a lot of confidence."

"Getting back to your father..."

"I'm done with him. I told you that."

"Are you sure you're done?"

She gazed at him through narrowed eyes. "How on earth can you ask me that?"

"Because you didn't throw the card away. Something inside you needs that connection to your father. Maybe because he's the only parent you have left."

She hated to admit there was some truth in his words. "Are you a shrink?"

"No, I'm a writer," he said with a dry smile.

"Seriously?" She was surprised that he'd actually revealed something about himself. "What do you write?"

"Novels mostly, a few short stories,

essays."

"Do you analyze your own life as much as you try to analyze others?"

"No, other people are far more interesting. So am I wrong, Liz? Do you have unfinished business with your father?"

She thought for a moment. "I loved my dad. Growing up, he was bigger than life. He was friendly, outgoing, charming, and handsome. He taught me how to ride a bike and hit a softball. He was good to me."

"There you go. You've spent a lot of time hating him, but you can't shake the bond between you no matter how much you want to."

"He needs to pay for what he did."

"He does," John agreed. "But you don't need to pay with him, and isn't that what you've been doing, Liz?"

"How do I stop?"

"Asking that question is the first step."

"And the second?"

"Chili cheese fries," he said with a grin as the waitress brought over their order. "We'll go from there."

"I should go home from here."

"The night is still young."

"Not really. It's almost midnight. My birthday is close to being officially over."

He reached across the table and put his hand over hers as she reached for a fry. "I'm not ready to say good-bye."

There was something very serious in his

expression now. Her hand tingled under his warm touch.

"I'm not, either," she murmured.

Chapter Seven

"Where are you taking me?" Carole asked, wondering why she'd agree to go anywhere with Alex. But here she was, sitting in his old jeep, in a designer cocktail dress. Her two worlds were colliding, and she was terribly afraid that she'd made a huge mistake. She'd stayed focused on her goals for almost two decades. Now wasn't the time to change, was it?

Alex turned down a dark alley that was very familiar.

"Really?" she asked. "You're taking me to Paradise Point?" It was a spot where teenagers went to drink and make out. And she'd done both there with Alex. He'd been such a good kisser, too. The random thought made her sit up a little straighter.

Alex didn't answer. Instead, he turned onto a dirt road and stopped the car at the edge of a bluff.

"I'm not getting out," she protested, as he opened his door. "I'm cold," she added when he walked around the car to open her door. "And this was a *parking* spot, remember?"

"Where I want to take you requires a walk. You'll survive."

"Says the man who's never had to walk in heels this high."

A small smile curved his lips. "They make your legs look damn good."

"Even at forty?"

"Better than ever." He helped her out of the car.

She clung to his hand as she stepped onto the rocky ground. "Can you believe we're this old, Alex?"

"I don't *feel* old. Do you?"

"Sometimes."

"Now?"

"Actually, no. Right now I feel about sixteen. Not that I want to go back there. I made a lot of mistakes at that age."

He smiled. "I'm not going to ask you to put a name on any of those mistakes."

"Good call. So where are we going?"

"You'll figure it out soon enough." He grabbed the edges of the coat he'd given her and buttoned it up. "Warm enough?"

His oversized coat was more than warm enough. In fact, she felt as if his arms were around her. And that thought brought another wave of heat. "I'm okay," she muttered, letting go of his hand. "I'll give you five minutes. That's all the time I have for the past."

"You always liked to set deadlines. Sometimes life doesn't go according to your timetable."

"Life – or you?" she asked dryly.

He tipped his head. "Both."

They walked away from the parking area down the path to the old run-down park that had once been a popular spot for the local kids. In fact, it was the park where she'd had her eighth birthday, the one where Alex had ruined her cake.

The seesaws were gone and most of the picnic tables were battered and falling apart. There were still two swings hanging from the metal rod and an old metal merry-go-round, but other than that it was just a very sad old place.

"It's even worse than I remembered," she muttered.

"They built a new park about two blocks from here, so none of the kids come here anymore. The view is still good, though."

She followed his gaze. The lights of the city spread out before them, reminding her of all the times she'd sat on top of one of the picnic tables, dreaming of one day being a part of those lights. "It is good," she said, feeling as if her real life were a million miles away.

"One of those lights belongs to you now."

"Yes. I have a beautiful house in the Marina. You can see the Golden Gate Bridge from the large bay window in my bedroom."

"Your mom said it was nice."

She walked over to the merry-go-round and put her hand on the cold metal. "I used to love this. I'd spin and spin and spin until I was so dizzy I couldn't think straight."

"I remember. Want to give it a try?"

She shook her head. "I'm already feeling off balance." She walked toward the swings and took a seat. She put her hands in the chain links and gave a little kick.

Alex came up behind her and gave her a push. "You always liked to swing high and fast, as if you could somehow catapult yourself into another dimension."

She smiled. He wasn't far off. She remembered wanting to watch her toes touch the sky. "Not tonight," she said, as he pushed her a little harder.

"You're more cautious now, aren't you?"

"I grew up."

"And lost your guts along the way?"

"I wouldn't say that – exactly." Although, there was a little truth to his words. "I don't want to lose what I have."

"Why would you?"

She didn't answer right away, then said, "My husband might leave me."

"Maybe you should leave him," Alex suggested.

"I couldn't do that. I have children. They need their father."

"Do they *have* their father?"

She defended him automatically.

"Blake's work is important. He could be a good leader."

"Is his work more important than his children? Than you?"

"I don't want to talk about him with you." She stopped the swing with her foot and jumped off, stumbling a little in her high heels.

Alex moved to her side. "Are you all right?"

"This was a mistake."

"Why?"

His warm breath blew against her cheek as he moved in closer. Her body tingled. This was Alex, the man she'd loved and adored for half her life. But that half of her life was over, she told herself. "I didn't come back here to find you, Alex," she said bluntly. "I came to find my mother."

"No, you didn't," he said with certainty in his gaze. "This trip wasn't about your mom or me. It was about you. You came back to find yourself."

His words struck home. "Do you think I'm lost?" she whispered.

"Don't you?"

"It's just that it's my birthday, and I'm forty, and I feel…" She couldn't find the right adjective.

"Lost," he finished.

She gazed into his eyes. "I thought I had what I always wanted, Alex."

"Even though you didn't have me?"

"I loved you, but that was a lifetime ago. We were on different paths. We wanted different things. We were kids."

"Just because we were young doesn't mean we didn't have real love, Carly."

"I wish you'd gone with me, Alex. But you were so determined to stay here."

"I couldn't go. My dad was sick, and you were too impatient to wait."

"That wasn't the only reason you stayed. You liked this neighborhood. This was your place, and it still is."

"That's true," he said with a nod. "I do care about this community, even more than I did back then. And maybe I used my father's illness as a reason to stay behind because deep down I knew we weren't going to end up together. I was going to be in your shadow. You were looking for a brighter star. You wanted more than I could give you."

"You hate me, don't you?"

"I've tried, Carly," he said finally. "You don't know how hard."

"My name is Carole. Everyone calls me that now."

"Everyone but me. You'll always be Carly to me – stubborn, exasperating, ambitious Carly."

"And you'll always be stubborn, exasperating, unambitious Alex. We're right back where we started."

He smiled. "In that case…"

His mouth covered hers in a hot, demanding kiss that rocked her back on her heels, stole her breath, and made the twenty years apart fade away. She was that young woman again – in love and lust, and her whole world was Alex. His arms wrapped around her waist and she pressed against his hard, solid chest, knowing every second that she should push him away but unable to find the strength.

It was Alex who finally broke away, the heat from their breath sending wisps of fog in the air between them. His eyes glittered in the moonlight, his jaw tightening as he took a step back.

"Damn," he said. "You can still kiss like no one else."

"So can you."

"You need to go home, Carly."

She stared back at him for a long moment. "That's the last thing I need."

* * *

"Where are we going now?" Liz asked as John helped her into yet another taxi after they'd finished off way too many chili cheese fries, washed down by too many cups of coffee. She was so wired, she felt impatient and a little reckless. Going home was not an option in her mind. In fact, she couldn't imagine going to sleep. She wanted to keep trying new things. She wanted to keep talking. Now that she'd told him about her parents, she had nothing left to hide, no reason to be guarded, and it was the first time in a long time she'd felt so free.

"Remember how I told you I was going to sail a boat under the Golden Gate Bridge on my birthday?" he asked.

"Yes."

He showed her his watch. "It's after midnight. It's no longer your birthday. It's mine."

"You're going to need to wait for daylight to set sail."

"We can do some pre-planning."

"We?" she queried. "This is your birthday resolution, not mine."

"I helped you celebrate. You don't want to return the favor?"

"I have no idea how to sail."

He smiled. "Neither do I. It will be a new experience, another chance to do what we don't ordinarily do. Your resolution has to last for at least more than one night."

"I never said that was my resolution," she said, smiling back at him because he was so damned good-looking that she couldn't help herself. If she wasn't careful, she'd find herself saying yes to anything he asked. Maybe that wouldn't be so bad; he hadn't steered her wrong yet.

"Do you have to work tomorrow?" John asked.

"No, I'm off."

"Then you don't have any reason to get home."

"Except that it's late and most people sleep during this time of the night."

"We're not most people, Liz – at least, not tonight."

"I'm never this spontaneous," she said. "I usually think long and hard before I act."

"You're not your father, Liz."

"Where did that come from?" she asked in surprise.

"I think you're afraid to be reckless, because that feeling reminds you of him."

"He was reckless. He hurt a lot of people. He didn't think about anyone but himself."

"And you think about everyone before yourself. It's a nice trait. But sometimes it's okay to be a little selfish. You're entitled."

"You're very good at reading people." She paused, tilting her head to one side. "You could be using me, conning me, and how would I know?"

"I guess you wouldn't, but you can leave any time you want."

"That's just it. You make it so I don't want to leave. Tell me something else about you, John. Tell me about the girl who broke your heart."

"How do you know there's a girl?" he asked.

"Because there is," she said, meeting his gaze. "You described her to me when we first met on the roof – the martini type. What happened to her?"

John sighed. "She picked someone else."

"Why? What's wrong with you?"

He grinned. "She had a fairly long list of what's wrong with me."

"Give me an example."

He hesitated for a long minute. "I used to get lost in my writing. I'd spend hours at the computer. She felt ignored."

"You could have changed that."

"I could have, but as I said, there was a long list. And I don't want her back, Liz. I saw her true colors, and they weren't pretty. Then again, I put her in a situation that would have been difficult for anyone."

"What situation was that?"

He hesitated. "It doesn't matter now. It's over. Let's talk about sailing."

She grabbed his hand and gave it a squeeze. "Fine. I'll let you change the subject, but just for the record, it doesn't sound like she was worth keeping."

He smiled. "You don't even know her."

"True, but I'm getting to know you, and you're very insightful, so I'm guessing whatever you figured out about her was pretty accurate. So far you've done a fairly good job assessing me."

"It comes from creating characters out of thin air. I'm used to digging for motivation, figuring out what makes someone tick."

"I know what makes you tick – the unknown," she said. "You crave excitement, change, new adventures. You don't want to do the same thing every day of your life."

"What would be the fun in that?"

"Maybe there's no fun, but there is stability. And there's a comfort that comes with predictability."

"That's what you want, Liz?"

"It's what I thought I wanted – until you came along and showed me that there was a big world out there I wasn't living in."

"You've only just started. You know that, right? I don't want you to quit after tonight."

"Well, maybe you'll have to stick around, make sure I don't."

A shadow crossed his face so quickly she would have missed it if she hadn't been watching him so intently. She realized she'd just put him in the awkward position of having to pretend there would be another night.

"I'm sorry. That came out wrong," she said quickly. "Sometimes I talk too much. I'm not expecting anything, John. You've showed me a great time, and when the sun comes up, I'm fully prepared to say goodbye."

"Well, that's not going to be for a few hours yet," he replied.

It wasn't what she'd wanted to hear, but

she left it alone. "Where's the boat?"

"In the marina. We can get on board, wait until dawn and then set sail. We can watch the sunrise from the waters of the bay."

"Okay, I'll go with you," she said, making a quick decision. Maybe she'd only have this one night, but she was going to make it count. "But, first I need to make a quick stop."

* * *

Liz's stop was an all-night drugstore a few blocks from the Marina. She wasn't going to John's boat without being a little more prepared. Leaving him in the taxi, she ran inside. Her first stop was at the greeting cards. She ran through some of the more amusing birthday cards and picked one appropriate for him. Next stop was to pick up condoms. She had no idea if he had any with him, but she certainly didn't, and the way the night was going, she wanted to be ready for anything. She might be acting on impulse, but she wasn't stupid.

After grabbing the condoms, she hurried around the corner, barreling right into another woman. The condoms and birthday card flew out of her hand, landing on the floor between them.

"Sorry," the woman said, as they both knelt down.

"It's okay," she replied, feeling a little embarrassed as the woman picked up the condoms and handed them to her. "Always be prepared," she said lightly. "It's my birthday. I'm thirty."

"It's my birthday, too," the woman said. "Thirty-five, but I don't think I'm going to have as much fun as you."

Liz picked up the box of children's cough medicine and handed it over. "Sick kid at home?" she asked sympathetically. "This is a good brand. It should knock that cough right out."

"Are you a mother?"

"No, I'm a nurse."

"Oh, well, thanks," the woman said as they both stood up. "I wasn't sure which one to buy. Have a nice night."

"I intend to," Liz said, taking her things to the counter.

As she returned to the taxi, John asked curiously, "What did you get?"

She smiled. "You're not the only one who gets to be mysterious."

"You're not going to tell me?"

"I might show you – if you're lucky."

Chapter Eight

Angela hurried into her apartment with her supplies from the drugstore. Colin had offered to make the trip, but she'd brought the girls home with her, and she intended to take care of them. Colin was reading in the living room and all was quiet.

"Are the girls asleep?"

"I have no idea. Laurel locked the bedroom door after you left. I think she's scared of me."

"They're in strange surroundings, and you weren't very welcoming earlier."

"You took me by surprise. You go out to get wine and come back with two homeless kids. I'm glad to see you only picked up cough medicine on this trip."

She was relieved to see that his anger had faded enough for him to joke a little.

"I know my behavior has been erratic, and I understand why you acted the way you did earlier. I'll go check on the girls."

He nodded, getting to his feet. "Then I guess I'll go to bed."

"I'll be in soon."

"Will you?" he asked, a doubtful note in his voice. "I feel like there's a huge wall between us that sprung up overnight."

"Not overnight, Colin. We both know that. Things have been strained for a while, and I realize that most of it is my fault. But not all of the distance between us is because of me."

"It's hard to know what to say to you that won't set you off," he said. "You're like a time bomb, and this birthday has brought everything to the boiling point. Your biological clock is in meltdown."

"It has been for years. It's not like I ever forget, Colin. I know you do. You fill up your days at work, and you go on, but it's always in the back of my mind. I just try to pretend that it's not, because I know it's hard for you to hear me complain all the time. Believe it or not, I annoy myself sometimes. I feel like such a whiner. I have so much, and yet I'm still not happy."

He walked across the room and gave her a tender kiss. "I know how hard this has been on you, Angie. I wish I could make you happy. I love you, Angie."

"I love you, too. And I need to make myself happy, Colin. It's not your responsibility."

"I'm your husband."

"And I'm your wife. I hate that my pain is hurting you, Colin. I just don't know what to do about it."

"We'll figure it out."

"I hope so."

"Good night," he said.

"Good night." A tiny seed of hope took root as he left the room. Maybe she and Colin could find a way to come back together again. But tonight she needed to focus on the girls.

She walked into the hall and knocked on the guest room door. "Laurel, it's me," she said quietly.

A minute later the door opened. As she walked into the room, Laurel scrambled back into the double bed she was sharing with Kimmie. Kimmie was already fast asleep, her stuffed bear tucked under her chin, her blonde hair glowing in the soft light from the lamp on the bedside table. She looked like a little angel. And Laurel looked like a young girl, not at all like the mugger who'd tried to steal her purse a few hours earlier.

"You should be asleep," she told Laurel, sitting in the chair next to the bed.

"I wanted to wait until you got back. Kimmie was scared."

"At least she's not coughing. I picked up some medicine," she added, setting the bag on the nightstand. "In case she wakes up." She paused as Laurel picked up the medicine and gave it a cursory look, as if to make sure it was something suitable for her sister. "You're used to watching over Kimmie, aren't you?"

"Ever since she was a baby," Laurel said. "I've been like her mother."

"Where is your mom, honey?"

"I don't know," Laurel said, honesty in her eyes. "She isn't usually gone this long."

"Where's your father?"

"I don't know who my dad is. Kimmie's father took off a while ago."

"So it's just you two and your mother. Does your mom work?"

"Sometimes she waitresses and we get free food."

"Do you know the name of the restaurant? Maybe they've heard from her."

"I don't remember the name."

She wasn't sure if that was true or if Laurel was trying to protect her mother, too. It was a big job taking care of a mother and a baby sister. "How old are you, Laurel?"

Laurel hesitated, then said. "Thirteen."

So young. Barely a teenager. "How often does your mom take off?"

"She was doing good for a while. Then she got a new boyfriend," she said with a disgusted sneer. "He liked to get high with her. And she started staying out all night with him."

Angela felt a surge of anger. The woman had two beautiful daughters, and she was neglecting them, putting them in jeopardy. It was criminal. The girls deserved a lot better.

"Can't we just stay here for a few days until my mom comes back?" Laurel asked. "We don't take up much space. And I can help you around the house. I can clean and I can cook some stuff."

She hated to erase the look of hope in Laurel's eyes, but she had to. "We don't know when your mom will be back, and you need more help than I can give you."

"They'll split us up. They always do. Families want Kimmie, because she's little and cute, but no one wants a teenager. I don't care so much for myself, but Kimmie gets so scared when we're apart. She needs me."

She thought Laurel probably needed Kimmie, too, even if she had too much bravado to say so. "I'll see if we can avoid a separation," she promised, having no idea if she could possibly make good on that promise. "But I can't keep you here."

"Because your husband doesn't like us?"

"Because it's not right. You don't belong to me. And you need a permanent solution, not a temporary one."

Laurel gave her a sad look. "We don't belong to anyone. No one wants us, not even our own mom."

"I'm sure she loves you. It sounds like she has a problem."

"Yeah, she always has a problem," Laurel said cynically. "How about you let us take off before your husband wakes up. You can say we ran away. No one has to know."

"I'll know," she said. "And I can't let

you go back to that apartment. It's not safe."

"It's safer than some of the places they send us."

Angela had no idea what the foster care system was like in San Francisco, but she could see the fear in Laurel's eyes and wished she could do something to make it go away. "I'll talk to the Social Worker. I'll make sure it's a good place," she said.

"Sure," Laurel said in a despondent voice.

"You have to have faith," she said, wondering where the words had come from. Hadn't Patrick said just the same thing to her earlier? And hadn't she told him that God didn't listen to her prayers, that faith had gotten her nowhere? She felt like a hypocrite.

But she also felt like fate had thrown her together with these two girls. She had to find a way to help them. Unfortunately, there was nothing she could do tonight. "You should try to get some sleep, Laurel."

"Do you think you could stay for a few minutes?" Laurel asked hesitantly.

"I can stay," she said, watching as Laurel slid deeper under the covers. "Are you warm enough?" Laurel nodded. She tucked the covers more closely around Laurel's small body. "My mother used to tuck me in really tight," she said.

"She sounds nice."

"She is nice." Angela thought about the

huge party her mother had just thrown her and felt a surge of guilt at how she'd acted. Her mother had always put her and her sisters before herself. She'd been incredibly blessed, and she'd had so much more love than the two little girls in front of her. She'd been very unappreciative.

"You're lucky."

"I am."

"My mom used to sing us to sleep when we were little," Laurel murmured. "It was a long, long time ago."

"You must miss her."

"I miss the way she used to be," Laurel replied, her eyelids drooping until she finally lost the battle and fell asleep.

Angela watched both girls sleep for about fifteen minutes, thinking that this guest room, which had always been designated as the nursery, finally had children in it. There was no baby in a crib, just two scared little girls in desperate need of a mother.

* * *

She'd been crazy to kiss Alex, Carly thought as they pulled into the parking lot behind Alex's bar. She was a forty-year-old married woman who'd never contemplated cheating on her husband. But this was Alex, her first love, which was also a problem. Alex wasn't a stranger. He was her past, he was someone who'd once been very important to her. He'd known her almost her entire life. And no one in her circle of friends went back that far.

"Where's your limo?" Alex asked.

"I have the driver's number. I said I'd call when I was ready to leave."

"You're ready," he said, cutting the engine. "It must be nice to have someone at your beck and call."

"Well, they're paid pretty well to be on call," she said dryly, turning in her seat.

"You can get anything as long as you're willing to pay for it," he said, an edge to his voice. "But not everything – not everyone – can be bought."

"I know that."

"Do you?"

The light in the parking lot cast long shadows along his face, making his features harder, edgier. There was a tension about him that was impossible to miss, and she wasn't exactly sure if it was all anger, or a mix of emotions.

"You should go," Alex added.

"You're kicking me out?"

"I think your slumming time is over."

"Now you're just being mean. Why?" She took a gamble. "Because that kiss meant something to you?"

"It didn't mean a damn thing," he said harshly, getting out of the car and slamming the door.

She drew in a breath as his anger ripped through her. But she wasn't going to let him intimidate her. She knew Alex as well as he knew her. Anger was his go-to emotion, even if he was just confused or hurt. She got out of the car and shut the door.

Alex hadn't moved too far away, which meant either he was being too polite and didn't want to leave her alone in the empty parking lot or that he wasn't quite as ready to say goodbye as he'd indicated.

She walked over to him. "That kiss felt like yesterday, Alex."

"But it's not yesterday. It's tonight, and tomorrow you'll go back to your life. Isn't that right?"

She was tempted to say no, but she was a realist. "Yes, that's right. But my life won't be the same now."

"I don't think you'll let one kiss derail your plans," he said dryly.

"I wouldn't have before tonight. But ever since I saw my humongous birthday cake with enough candles to start a three-alarm fire, I've been questioning everything about myself. I locked away the past so it wouldn't distract me, but the past is right in front of my face now, and I'm not so sure where I'm going to go from here."

"You? The girl who was always certain of her destiny?"

"Ironic, I know."

"What do you want, Carly?"

She searched for the right words. "I want to be happy."

"And what will make you happy?"

"Would it scare you if I said *you*?" she asked daringly, wondering how she could really make that happen. She was married. She had children. She was forty years old. She couldn't toss everything away for a man. Hell, when she was eighteen, she hadn't been able to throw everything away for Alex.

"It would scare me if you really meant it," he said, meeting her gaze. "But you don't. I didn't belong in your world twenty years ago, and I don't belong there now."

"You're not some loser, Alex. I don't think of you that way."

"Why? Because now you know I own a bar?"

"I *never* thought of you that way."

"Of course you did, Carly. You didn't think I could give you the life you wanted, so you bailed on us."

"Because you didn't want that life," she snapped. "You wanted exactly what you got. You were just as stubborn as I was only in a different way."

"Even if that's true, I know that tonight is just a moment of temporary insanity for you – a sweet trip down memory lane, where you remember the good stuff and none of the bad."

"Believe me I have not forgotten the

bad," she said. "I did not have the great family that you did."

"I know your father's abuse left a scar, but you did have a pretty good mom, even if she wasn't well educated, sophisticated, or rich."

"You make me sound so shallow."

"I'm just stating the facts. Tomorrow you'll go back to your real life, and tonight will be just another memory that you'll eventually lock away again."

"What if I don't want that life anymore?" she asked, voicing the doubts that had been plaguing her for more than just a night.

"I'd be shocked if that were true."

"I've been feeling restless for years. Tonight was just the tipping point."

"Then make a change. But don't involve me. I can't let you back in, Carly. I know you too well. Tomorrow you'll wake up, and your husband will kiss you, probably buy you an expensive diamond necklace to make up for whatever he's been doing, and you'll move right along with your life."

"Do you think I can be bought with a diamond necklace?" she asked, a little hurt by his words, even though she couldn't deny that Blake's generosity with money was one of the things she loved about him.

"You tell me."

"I can't – not anymore. I'll admit that I

wanted money when I was younger. I wanted the big house, and the rich husband, the clothes, and the vacations. I wanted my kids to have more than I had. And I did everything I could to make that happen. But I never realized that those things don't make a family. You can love them, but they don't love you back. I'm lonely, Alex. I have this hole in my soul, and it gets worse every year."

"Then leave him. Change your life. You have the guts, and you have the money. What's stopping you?"

"I'm afraid of walking away and finding out the hole is still there."

Alex stepped forward and tilted up her chin with his fingers. "That's the smartest thing you've ever said. Because no matter where you go, how much money you make, how many expensive dinners you eat, you can't escape from yourself. And until you figure out a way to be both Carly and Carole, you're never going to be complete."

She caught her breath, his words striking deep and hard. She'd never thought of herself as two people, but wasn't that exactly who she was? Wasn't her life divided into halves? "How do you know me so well?"

"Because, God help me, I've always loved you – all of you, the good, the bad, the confused…"

"Why didn't you ever come after me,

Alex? Why didn't you fight for me?"

He shook his head. "It wouldn't have done any good. You were and always have been one stubborn woman." He kissed her hard on the lips. "Go home, Carly. Go back to your life and make yourself happy. I have every confidence you can do it."

"What about you? What are you going to do?"

"I'm already happy."

She smiled at his simple, blunt statement, hearing nothing but truth in his words. But then, Alex had never needed that much. "I'm glad, Alex. Really I am. I never wanted to hurt you, even though I know I did."

"You were on a quest. And you did well for yourself." He met her gaze. "You can be Carly, you know. She wasn't so bad. In fact, she could be a lot of fun when she wasn't worrying so much about controlling every aspect of her life. Maybe your kids and husband need to get to know her."

"I can't imagine what they'd think."

"It's time to find out."

"Thanks, Alex." She turned to leave, then paused. "You still owe me a birthday cake. One of these days, I'm going to collect."

* * *

Carole didn't go home; she went to pick

up her mother from work. Nora looked tired and worn out as she slid into the limo.

"I wasn't sure you'd really come," Nora said.

"I wouldn't leave you to find a ride at one in the morning."

"Well, I figured you'd send someone," her mother said with a cynical note in her voice.

Before tonight's events, she probably would have done just that. "You look exhausted. Why don't you use the money I sent you and quit this job?"

"Your aunt needs the help."

"Then give her the money and let her hire someone else."

"Don't worry about it, Carly. I'm fine."

"You always told me that – even when I found you with a bloody nose and a gash on your head from where Dad knocked you into the cabinets. But you weren't fine then, and you aren't now."

Nora gave her a disbelieving look. "It's a little late to care, isn't it? I've been doing just fine on my own the last ten years."

"I should have contacted you before now. I feel badly about all the time that's passed. In the beginning I was just so mad at you, I couldn't pick up the phone, and then the years went by, and we were always busy with Blake's family, and it seemed safer to leave you out of the equation."

"Well, at least you're being honest."

Nora paused as the limo stopped in front of her building. "Thanks for the ride."

"I'm coming up," she said. "I didn't wait around all night just to give you a ride."

Nora gave her a thoughtful look and then shrugged. "It's your call."

"I won't need you again tonight," she told the limo driver. "Thanks."

She followed her mother upstairs and into the apartment. While her mother used the restroom, she moved into the kitchen and checked the refrigerator and cupboards. She was hungry. She'd barely eaten at the party, and her stomach was rumbling. As her gaze lit on a familiar package of cookies, she couldn't help smiling. She pulled them out, along with a carton of milk, and set them on the kitchen table. Then she grabbed two glasses. She'd just finished pouring the milk when her mother came back into the room.

"Oreos and milk – your favorite treat," Nora said, giving her a sad smile.

"And still yours apparently."

"I can't seem to shake it."

She sat at the table as Nora did the same. Pulling out a cookie, she dipped it halfway into the milk and then took a bite. It tasted delicious but along with the sweet chocolate came a host of memories, all the times they'd shared cookies and milk and heart-to-heart conversations. Before she'd become a bratty, rebellious teenager, they'd been fairly close.

"Why did we ever stop this?" she murmured.

"You went on a diet in high school and said the cookies were too fattening," Nora replied.

"Did you hate me when I was a teenager?"

"You were a challenge, but I always loved you. Do you have cookies and milk with your kids?"

She shook her head, heaviness settling around her heart. "I think the nanny used to."

"Well, I'm sure you do other things with them."

"I'm not a very good mother," she confessed. "I've made a lot of mistakes."

"All mothers do. Lord knows I screwed up a bunch of times."

"I shouldn't have been so hard on you."

"I let you down, Carly. I know that. And it wasn't just on your thirtieth birthday that I made a fool of myself; I screwed up long before that. You're not the only one who regrets the past."

She looked into her mother's eyes, so similar to her own, and felt a wave of emotion. "You used to say it was you and me against the world."

"It used to feel that way. It wasn't easy raising you when your dad was around. He could be sweet and then so damn mean. After he left, it was safer, but it was harder without his income. I wanted you to have all the things you wanted, but I just didn't know how to give them to you. I didn't have your smarts, your will, or your determination. I'm proud of you, Carly. Proud of everything you've accomplished. Maybe you were able to get to where you are now because you let me go." She took a breath. "I used to tell myself that to make myself feel better."

Carole let out a sigh, realizing how much she'd hurt her mother. She'd always justified her behavior by saying her mother deserved it.

"You deserved more than my silence," she said. "You did your best to make things right for me, and I do have happy memories. I just don't like to admit that. But tonight I had an epiphany. I looked around a crowded ballroom and realized that no one there really knew me. My kids took off before I blew out the candles. Blake only participated because it was a great networking event. I knew something had to change, and that something was me."

"So you came home."

"I wanted to see you. I wanted to remember what I'd tried so hard to forget."

"And now?"

"I want to do better. I don't know exactly how."

"No twelve-point plan? That's so unlike you."

She acknowledged her mother's

knowing smile. "No plan – not yet, anyway. But one thing I know for sure. I want you to be a part of my life."

"I'd like that very much. What about Blake?"

"He'll have to deal."

"Now, that sounds like my Carly."

"It does, doesn't it?" she said, feeling a wave of new energy. "I can do it. I can change my life. I'm forty. I'm starting a new decade. I think it's going to be a good one."

"I do, too. So what did you do tonight while you were waiting for me?" Nora asked.

She smiled, knowing that her mother was the only person to whom she could tell the truth. "Well, I kissed Alex."

Her mother choked on her cookie and started coughing.

"Are you all right?" she asked.

"I don't think I heard you right."

"I should be sorry, but I'm not. It woke me up."

Her mother gave her a worried look. "You need to be careful, Carly. You have a lot to lose."

"I know. But I realized tonight that I've been trying so hard not to lose what I have that I didn't realize I'd already lost a lot."

Nora sighed. "I hope you know what you're doing."

"I haven't figured out what I'm doing yet. But I know where I need to start."

Chapter Nine

Liz gazed up at the stars in amazement. Tonight seemed to be a night of stunning views, first from the roof of the hospital, then from Potrero Hill, and now from a boat in the Marina. Away from the city lights, there was an endless array of stars, and along with those sparkling lights came a feeling of anticipation.

Lowering her gaze from the night sky, she called to John, "Did you get lost?"

"Be right there," he yelled back.

She settled against soft, billowing pillows on a bench seat at the back of the boat. She'd imagined something small with a big sail, not this luxurious yacht with a large stateroom down below and a fully stocked galley. John's friend obviously had some money.

John came up the stairs and set a tray on the table in front of her. Two steaming cups of coffee greeted her as well as a small plate of chocolates.

"More food?" she said with a groan. "I'm definitely going to need that diet resolution after tonight."

"Hey, it's your birthday."

"We passed from my birthday to yours a few hours ago. Speaking of which–" She reached into her bag and pulled out the card she'd purchased earlier. She handed to him. "For you."

"This is what you got at the store?" he asked as he opened the envelope. He read the sentiment and laughed. "*Growing old is mandatory; growing up is optional.*" He grinned at her. "Are you saying I'm not a grown up?"

"I'm saying I hope you don't ever lose your spirit. Your joy in living is contagious, John. If that makes you Peter Pan, then I'll be Wendy. Because when I'm with you, I feel like I'm flying." She put her hands on his shoulders and gazed into his eyes, seeing the same glitter of desire that she was feeling – but he was fighting it. "What's wrong?"

"I don't want you to have regrets."

"I won't," she said with a certainty that surprised even her. "I want this. I want you. You're my birthday wish."

He shook his head. "You didn't wish for me."

"Didn't I?" she murmured. "You showed up at just the right time." She frowned. "Why are you resisting? Aren't you the man who lives for new experiences? I could be fantastic in bed."

He grinned. "I'm sure you would be. But I don't want to hurt you. You're not a hook-up kind of girl."

"I'm not asking you for anything. No promises. No plans. Nothing."

"It's easy to say that now…"

"Now is all that matters. Who knows what the future will bring? But we have tonight. I've been cautious too long." She pressed her lips against his mouth, then said, "Let's fly."

His arms came around her waist, pulling her up sharply against his body. The easygoing man who'd been so charming and lighthearted suddenly seemed intense and even a little dark. But she wanted his intensity. She wanted the sudden emotion swirling between them, because no matter what she'd said, this wasn't just a hook-up. She wanted to get past John's barriers the way he'd gotten past hers. She wanted to connect on a deep, emotional level. She wanted to fall in love.

* * *

Angela stared at the half-finished paintings in the room across the hall from where the girls slept. She hadn't been able to paint anything to completion in almost three years. It was as if her subconscious refused to put an end to anything – including her dream of having a baby.

She stepped up to the easel, tracing the lines with the tip of her finger. Her last effort had been this landscape. It had come out of a dream like so many of her pictures – a beautiful park, a tranquil pond, a couple of ducks by the waterfall, and in the distance a playground, a baby stroller... She drew in a breath and let it out. That was where she'd stopped. She hadn't been able to finish, because there was no baby in that stroller and there was a good chance there never would be.

The door behind her opened, and she whirled around in surprise. While it wasn't a hard and fast rule, in recent years she'd made it pretty clear to Colin that she didn't want him in her studio. He'd been hurt at first, because he'd always supported her art, but after seeing her half-finished paintings, he'd been happy enough to leave. They'd just reminded him how stuck she was when it came to anything that distracted her from her dream of having a child.

It wasn't Colin in the doorway; it was Kimmie.

"Honey, are you all right?" she asked quickly.

Kimmie held her bear in one hand while she rubbed her eye with the other. "I woke up."

"Do you need something to drink?"

She shook her head as she walked toward the painting. "This is pretty. Did you draw it?"

"I did."

Kimmie tilted her head. "How come there aren't any people in it?"

"It's not done yet," she said.

"Maybe you could put me in the picture," Kimmie suggested.

"That's a good idea."

"Laurel doesn't let me go to the park. She says we have to stay in the house while Mommy is gone."

"Your sister is very smart. You should listen to her."

"But I like the swings, and all the other kids go to the park. Maybe Mommy will take me when she comes back."

The hope in Kimmie's voice made Angela sad. The little girl might still have faith in her mother now, but how long would it take for her to lose that faith? It was clear that Laurel had already lost hope. She hated to see that happen to Kimmie, too.

"If my mom doesn't come back, maybe you could take us," Kimmie added. A sudden burst of coughing followed her words.

"I'd like that," she said. Kimmie had no idea how drastically her life might change in the morning, but now wasn't the time to tell her. She needed to sleep. "Let's get you back to bed."

Kimmie slipped her tiny hand into hers with a trusting smile, and followed her to the guest room. Laurel was fast asleep, so Angela gave Kimmie some cough medicine, got her settled and stayed next to the bed until Kimmie fell asleep. Then she left, but instead of heading to her bedroom, she returned to the studio.

For several long minutes she stared at the painting … and then she reached for brushes and paint. She had no conscious thought of how she would finish the picture, but as soon as she began to paint, the figures took shape.

An hour or so later, she heard another sound, and this time it was Colin in the doorway. She wondered how long he'd been there, because there was an odd look on his face. "You're painting again," he said.

"I felt suddenly inspired."

He walked into the room and saw the children and families who now populated the painting. "You said you couldn't give anyone a happy ending until you had one," he said, reminding her of something she'd once said in a fit of anger and resentment.

"It's just a picture."

"It's more than that. It's you. It's your vision. You're so talented, Angela. Do you know how good this is?"

Warmth spread through her at his compliment.

"You've always been so much more than just a woman who couldn't have a baby," he added. "I wish you could see that the way I do."

"I think I'm starting to," she said slowly, unwilling to completely let go of the desire to procreate that had held her in a tight grip for the last eight years. "I forgot how much I love to paint."

"Keep going. Finish it," he told her.

"I will," she promised.

After he left, she painted with even more enthusiasm, picking up one discarded picture after another, adding new shades, mixing colors, taking chances. When she finally set down her brush, she was exhausted. She stepped back in wonder, amazed at what she'd done. None of the paintings had been completed as she'd originally intended. But they were good. Maybe even better than she'd imagined.

* * *

"It's almost time for that sail," Liz said sleepily, as she nestled against John's broad shoulder. After making love twice, they'd fallen asleep on the narrow bench under the stars, a blanked wrapped around them like a cocoon.

"I don't think I can move," he said, as he stroked her bare back with his hand.

"That's okay with me," she replied, more than content to stay where they were.

"No regrets?" he asked.

She lifted her head and gave him a thoughtful look. In the dawn light, he looked endearingly handsome with his morning stubble. But there was something in his eyes that gave her pause. "No regrets for me. What about you?"

He smiled. "Are you kidding? You were amazing."

"*We* were amazing," she corrected. "I can't quite believe how all this came to be, John. One minute I'm having a pathetic party of one on the roof of the hospital and the next minute I'm dancing, drinking, having the time of my life. It's crazy how fast life can change. Thank God you decided to get some air last night and come up to the roof. Otherwise, I never would have met you."

"Fate," he said, his fingers gently pushing her hair off her face.

"It feels like that," she said, gazing into his eyes. "I have a feeling my thirties are going to be better than my twenties."

"I think you're going to have a fantastic life, Liz."

His words didn't make it sound like he was planning to be a part of her fantastic life. Well, what did she expect? He'd told her the night before that he couldn't make any promises. She forced a smile to her lips, unwilling to let him see that she was already emotionally attached to him. "It is going to be great."

He nodded, but there was something unsettling in his somber gaze.

"What's wrong?" she asked.

"Not a thing."

She frowned. "I'm trying not to be a girl and ask a lot of questions, but your mood is worrying me."

"Don't try to be anything but what you are, Liz. That's more than good enough." He paused. "I don't think I'm going to be able to take that sail this morning."

"Why not?"

"I have somewhere else I need to be."

"Since when?"

"Since I realized that I need to keep an appointment I wasn't sure about."

"That's vague," she said with a frown.

He smiled. "I don't want you to worry, Liz. Tonight meant a lot to me. Meeting you was – life-changing."

Her nerves tingled at the look in his eyes. "No one has ever said that about me."

"Well, it's true. You're different."

"Now, *that* I've heard."

"Different in a good way," he said. "You're smart, honest, completely without pretension. And you've survived a lot."

"I don't want to just survive any more. I want to live the way you do, John. I want to make big goals and reach for the stars. I don't want to settle for someone who isn't right for me just so I won't be alone. I don't want to be content with a glass that's only half full. I don't want to spend so much time worrying about not having a boyfriend or being married or having children that I don't enjoy the life I'm actually having."

He smiled. "You got all that from a night of champagne and dancing?"

"I got all that from you. Your enthusiasm is contagious."

"So is your rediscovered fighting spirit. I'm impressed."

"Hopefully it will last." She paused, noting the shadow in his gaze once again. "Do you want me to leave?"

"No."

"Can you tell me what's going on in your head?

"That's not a conversation for tonight."

"It's pretty much morning."

"But not quite," he said, pulling her down for a kiss.

* * *

Liz woke to the heat of the sun on her face. She blinked against the bright light, taking a minute to gather her wits about her. She was naked, and she was alone. Abruptly, she sat up. "John?"

There was no answer.

She wrapped the blanket around her and walked down the stairs. The galley and stateroom were empty, and so was the bathroom.

Worry followed her back up the stairs. She grabbed her clothes and dressed quickly, wondering where John had gone. When she reached for her shoes, she saw the box on one of the bench seats. There was a cup of coffee and a bag of bagels and cream cheese inside.

There was also a note.

She sat down and opened the folded piece of paper, her hand shaking as her uneasiness increased. She wasn't an expert at one-night stands, but she didn't think that John taking off could possibly be a good sign, even if he had left her bagels and coffee. Something had been going on with him last night. Something not even his charming smile could completely hide.

Liz,

Sorry to take off without saying good-bye, but it's easier this way. At least for me, and you might not know this about me, but I can be selfish. Last night I didn't go up to the roof to get some air. I went up with one crazy thought – to throw myself off.

She drew in a quick breath of shock, then forced herself to keep reading.

You assumed I was there because my father died. But that wasn't the only reason. My dad actually passed away six months ago, and I've been mourning him. But I was in the hospital yesterday for a pre-surgical appointment. Three weeks ago I was diagnosed with a brain tumor. The doctors said my only option was surgery. It's risky, and there's a good chance I won't wake up, and even if I do, I might be irrevocably damaged. I realized that every dream I'd ever had was in jeopardy. I might never sail under the Golden Gate Bridge. I might never

*even walk or talk again. I might not be me.
The idea of not being able to live life on my
terms sent me up to that roof last night. And
then I met you.*

*At first, I was just postponing the
inevitable. You wanted a crazy, wonderful
night, and I wanted the same. I wanted to go
out with a bang. I wanted to take the boat
and sail into the horizon and maybe never
come back. But somewhere in the night, I
realized that I didn't want to die. I didn't
want to give up without a fight – the way
your mom did. I hadn't thought about the
people I'd be leaving behind. I don't have
much family, but I do have some friends, and
they'd hate me for taking the easy way out. I
know you think I changed you, but the truth
is that you changed me.*

I was scheduled for surgery this
morning. I decided to keep the appointment,
to fight for my life.

*I don't want you to worry about me, Liz.
You're the type of woman who would stick
through thick or thin. My last girlfriend took
off the day after I got the diagnosis. I didn't
really blame her. This is my problem, my
challenge. I want you to go out and live your
life the way you were meant to. And one of
these days, I hope we'll meet again. In the
meantime, I want you to be happy.*

Tears streamed down her cheeks as she
realized exactly what he was saying. How
could he possibly have a brain tumor? He'd

shown no signs of illness the night before. But she'd felt his desperation the last time they'd made love. It was as if he had been trying to make it the best it could ever be. Maybe because he'd thought it was truly the last time. Damn. She blinked away the tears so she could read the rest of his letter.

P.S. I know you're thinking right now that you need to find me and that you want to help me. Don't come. Don't waste your day. I want you to go to Faith's Fancies. It's a great little bakery in North Beach, and they're going to have a special cake waiting for you. I want you to have it – to replace the one I made you drop. That's what you can do for me.

And stop crying, Liz. If I hadn't met you, I would have missed out on one of the greatest nights of my life. I truly have no regrets.

John

She set down the letter, unable to stop crying as he'd requested. It amazed her that he knew her so well, anticipating every move she would want to make, because she really did want to find him. She wanted to be there for him. And she would.

Jumping to her feet, she realized that the only reason he would have been on that roof was because his doctor was in the hospital. She'd find him. She had to do more for him than just eat a birthday cake.

Chapter Ten

Angela woke to the smell of bacon and the sound of laughter. Throwing on her bathrobe, she walked into the kitchen to find Colin making breakfast for Laurel and Kimmie. The girls were laughing, and Colin had a big grin on his face. The scene seemed so surreal, so close to so many of her dreams, that she had to blink her eyes a few times to make sure she wasn't imagining it.

"Colin is making animal pancakes," Laurel said, catching her eye.

"He made me a bear just like Mr. Bear," Kimmie said with delight, her mouth half full of pancake.

She moved around the island where Colin was getting ready to flip another batch of cakes. "Thank you for doing this."

"My way of saying I'm sorry for not being very supportive when you first brought the girls home last night. We're a team. We've always been a team, and we stick together, no matter what."

"I like the sound of that."

He gave her a warm smile. "Now, what will you have? Bunnies or bears? I can't make much else."

"I'll take a bear," she said, grabbing a

plate.

Over breakfast, the conversation was light and easy. Laurel and Kimmie obviously felt more comfortable now with Colin, and it was clear that Kimmie liked to talk. She related endless tales about school and friends and people in their building, and even a few revealing details about her mother. Laurel tried to shush her on occasion, but Kimmie would jump back in again five minutes later, making her big sister sigh.

"It's okay," she told Laurel as Kimmie left the table to use the bathroom. "We want to help you."

"But you said you're calling the police."

"First we're going to talk to a friend of mine," Colin interjected.

She gave her husband a surprised look. "We are?"

"Yes." He paused. "Laurel, do you mind if I speak to Angela alone for a few minutes?"

"I'll check on Kimmie," Laurel said, her eyes still worried, but there was a tiny bit of hope in her gaze as well.

"I called Rebecca Hensley," he said when they were alone.

"Paul's wife?" she asked, referring to Colin's coworker.

"Rebecca works for the Department of Children and Families. She said we might be able to apply for emergency foster parent status, which could still take some time, but she's going to come over later this morning and talk to us."

"Are you serious?" she asked in astonishment. "You want to be a foster parent?"

"Possibly. I think it's an option we should explore."

"We never considered that."

"So we'll do it now. Watching you with the girls reminded me of how great you are with kids, how lucky someone would be to have you as a mother."

Her eyes blurred with emotion. "That's so sweet, Colin. But you're talking about a huge commitment."

"Like I said, we're a team. And I let you down when I quit. But I'm back in the game now."

She felt an overwhelming wave of relief. "I don't know what to say, except I love you. And I'm glad you're not giving up on me, on our dreams."

"Exactly, our dreams. For a while I forgot how much I wanted kids, too. But I do. I can't waste my pancake making skills on just you."

She smiled through her happy tears. "You're incredible, do you know that?"

He smiled. "I try. But I have to warn you that this could get very messy. We don't know about anything about Laurel and Kimmie's mother. She could be a good person who needs a little help to get back on her feet and be a mother again."

"That would be the best scenario," she said quickly. "That's what I would want for them. They need their mother. You might find that difficult to believe, because I've been so crazy lately, but I'm not so far gone as to think I'd be a better substitute than someone's biological mother."

"I don't find it difficult to believe," he interrupted. "I know what a big heart you have, Angie. But it's also more than likely that their mother is in serious trouble. Why else would she have left her kids?"

"I don't know."

"We need to find out." He paused. "We have a lot to offer a child – even if it's not a baby or it's not Laurel and Kimmie. There's some child out there who needs us. The real question is can you look beyond having a baby yourself to adopting?"

"I didn't think I could – until I met them. All along I've been so focused on being pregnant that I forgot the most important part – the years that come after the baby is born. I want to be a mother. I want a house with children in it. I want kids around this table and bunny pancakes and mornings just like this."

"I want that, too. And we can cash in the cruise tickets and try IVF again."

"You're amazing. But I have to tell you this, Colin. If at the end of all this, it's just you and me, I'll still be the luckiest woman on earth. And I'll have no regrets."

He smiled. "We're not going to end up alone. We're going to make it happen." He took her hand and gave it a squeeze. "One way or another, we're going to make a family."

* * *

Carole walked into the big house she shared with Blake and her children, and the first thing she noticed was the silence. The large kitchen was empty, and no dishes sat in the sink. Obviously the kids were still at their friends' houses – which left Blake. She wondered if he'd stayed at the hotel as they'd planned, if he'd come home... or if he'd spent the night with someone else. She'd certainly made it easy for him to do just that.

She climbed the stairs and walked into the master bedroom suite. Blake was wearing charcoal gray slacks and buttoning up a dress shirt.

He gave her a cool look. "Finally decided to come home?"

"Yes." She sat down on the edge of the bed. "Are you going to ask me where I've been?"

"Do I want to know?" he countered, reaching for a tie.

"I went to see my mother."

"Why?" he asked, as he slung the tie around his neck.

He wasn't even looking at her, but rather at his reflection in the mirror, and the familiarity of this moment struck her hard. She'd been staring at the back of his head for far too long.

"I needed a reality check. Could you look at me, Blake?"

"I'm in a hurry, Carole. We have lunch with the Dunsmuirs in less than an hour. Why don't you get changed, and we'll have this conversation later?"

He still hadn't looked at her. "I'm not going to lunch."

"Don't be ridiculous. You always come with me. This is important. They have a lot of money to donate to my campaign."

"Michael has a football game today. Sophie is cheerleading. It's homecoming. I want to go to the game."

Finally, he turned around, confusion in his eyes. "Are you serious? It's a football game. And Michael rarely gets into the game; he's only a sophomore."

"If he does, I want to be there. I invited my mother to come as well."

"Are you crazy?"

"Actually, I'm feeling remarkably sane."

"Is this about Krystal?" he asked shortly. "I told you there's nothing going on there."

She drew in a deep breath. "I'm not stupid, Blake. I don't know if you've had an affair or if you're contemplating one, but you crossed the line last night."

"She was flirting with me; I flirted back. Big deal. Her father is going to donate a lot of money to my campaign."

"So you're selling yourself to her?"

"I'm not having an affair," he said flatly. "Believe me or not, I don't care."

"Why don't you care?" she challenged. "Why doesn't it matter how I feel – what I think?"

He sighed in frustration. "Are you PMSing, Carole? Or are you just pissed that you're forty?"

"This is not about my hormones or my age – well, maybe a little about my age," she amended. "Because I certainly don't want to waste the next decade living the way I've been living."

"What are you talking about? We have a good life."

"We barely touch each other. It's been months since we've made love."

"We've been busy. Look, we're a fantastic team together. There is no limit to our future. We could be in the Governor's mansion one day, maybe even the White House. That's what we need to focus on. And you know that, because you've always been able to see the dream as clearly as I did."

His eyes glittered with ambition, an ambition she'd once shared and found intoxicating. But she was no longer drunk on dreams. She was stone cold sober and forty years old. She didn't want to waste the rest of her life chasing a fantasy. "I want you to be successful, Blake, but not at the expense of our children. I need to spend more time with them."

"They're teenagers. They're practically grown." He frowned at her. "Look, I get that you're having a midlife crisis. But I've given you everything you ever wanted, and you're being ungrateful."

"You have given me a lot," she admitted. "But what I want now is family, love, time together. I can't give you a hundred and fifty percent of myself anymore. I need to focus on the children, on my mother, and on me."

"So what are you saying?" he challenged. "You want out?"

She was shocked that he'd actually asked the question. "I don't know."

"It won't come cheap."

"Is that a threat?"

"A fact. If you bail on me, I'll have to work hard to rebuild my reputation."

She shook her head in amazement. "Do you know how cold and cruel you sound?"

"Do you know how stupid you're being to want to throw away this incredible life for your mother?"

"It's not just about her. It's about the children."

"They're fine."

"You barely see them."

"I provide for them – and for you. What do you think you would do without me? You haven't held down a job in twenty years. You're not qualified to do anything but be my wife. Without me, you'll end up just like your mother. Is that what you want?"

There had been a time when his words would have sent her into sheer terror, but somewhere in the night she'd rediscovered her backbone.

She tried to inject a little calm into their conversation. "I'm not asking for you to give up your dreams, Blake, just readjust a little bit – for me, for the kids." She paused. "It's much easier for a good family man to get elected."

His gaze narrowed. "Now you're threatening me?"

"As you said, I'm just stating a fact." She hadn't mixed with power brokers for almost two decades without having learned a few tricks of her own. She wasn't sure she could fix what was wrong with her marriage and her family, but she was determined to at least try, if not for herself then for her kids. Sophie and Michael needed a father, too.

"I can't reschedule lunch. They're flying back to New York tonight." He sighed. "You go to the game. I'll tell them you're not feeling well."

"You could just tell them I needed to be with my kids," she said dryly.

"Since you've never needed to do that before, I doubt they'd believe me," he said cynically.

She met his knowing gaze. "I know I'm changing right in front of you, but it's actually been happening for a lot longer than you know. I haven't been happy, Blake. And I haven't been as good a mother as I should have been. Seeing my mom last night reminded me of that."

"Your mother is a hell of an example. She's still not welcome in my house."

"Our house," she corrected, getting to her feet. "And she is welcome here. Because she's my mother and I never should have turned my back on her. I feel so badly about my behavior."

He shook his head. "I don't have time for this. I'll see you later."

As Blake left, she waited for the doubts to come, for the urge to run after him and make things right. She could still change clothes and catch up to him at lunch, tell the Dunsmuirs she was feeling better. But when she got up and went into her closet, she found herself reaching for jeans and a T-shirt, and when she left the house, she headed to the private high school her kids attended. She had a feeling that they'd be just as surprised by her decision to come as

Blake had been.

She arrived at the game fifteen minutes later. She walked along the front of the grandstand, pausing in front of the cheerleaders as they finished their routine. When they tossed their pom-poms high into the air, she started clapping.

Sophie saw her and stopped abruptly, shock on her face. Then she walked over to the fence. "Mom? What's wrong? Has something happened?"

"Everything is fine," she said. "I just wanted to watch you and Michael. Has he gotten in the game yet?"

"Not yet," Sophie said, disbelief in her eyes. "Are you sure there's nothing wrong? Where's Dad?"

"He went to lunch with the Dunsmuirs."

"Without you? You always go with him."

"Not any more. I want to watch you cheer."

"Why?"

"Because you're my daughter."

Are you okay?"

"Yes," she said with a laugh. "Go on, show me what you can do."

"All right, I will," Sophie said slowly. "Thanks for coming."

"I love you, Sophie," she said, realizing how long it had been since she'd said the words.

Sophie flushed and muttered something,

then ran back to join her friends.

Carole took a seat on the bleachers, realizing sadly that she knew none of the parents of her children's friends. One day at a time, she thought, echoing her mother's favorite mantra. She might have messed up the last decade, but today was the beginning of the next.

* * *

Liz ran into the hospital, heading straight for the surgery department. One of her friends, Peggy Harrington, was working the nurse's station. "John – I mean Eric –" she said in a rush. "A man with a brain tumor. I need to know if he's in surgery. I don't know his last name." It occurred to her how little she did know about him, but she knew the important things, and she knew that he was important.

"What's going on?" Peggy asked, arching an eyebrow in surprise.

"Is he here?" she said.

"There's a man by the name of Eric Connors in surgery," Peggy said, checking the computer screen. "Is that who you're talking about?"

"Yes. Has he already been sedated?" She really wanted to talk to him before he went under, to reassure him, to let him know she was there offering support. She didn't give a damn that he'd requested she ignore the whole thing was happening.

"They got started about ten minutes ago," Peggy said.

"Who's the doctor?"

"Dr. Reston."

"He's good, right?" She didn't work in surgery, but she'd heard that Sam Reston was one of the best neurosurgeons on staff.

"He's excellent. Why are you so worried about someone whose last name you don't know?" Peggy inquired.

"We met last night." She couldn't begin to explain their whirlwind relationship to Peggy, especially not now while she was so worried. "I didn't know he was having surgery this morning."

"We were a little surprised when he actually showed up. He's cancelled twice before."

"What's the prognosis with surgery?"

"Less than fifty-fifty," Peggy said somberly. "It's such a shame. He's a young guy. I hope he makes it."

"He has to make it," she muttered. "I'm going to wait."

"It will be hours, Liz."

She knew that, but she needed to be close by. It didn't make logical sense because John wouldn't know, but she would know. The guy had turned her life upside down and made her see herself in a whole new light. The least she could do was give him support. "I need to be here," she said.

"I'll be in the waiting room."

"I'll let you know as soon as it's over," Peggy promised. "You really like this guy, don't you?"

"I do," she admitted. "And I don't want to lose him."

She blew out a breath and walked into the waiting room as Peggy answered the phone. While the hospital was her second home, she wasn't used to being in this position, and she didn't like it. She also didn't like the fact that she was so invested in a man she'd known less than twenty-four hours, but she was emotionally attached to him, for better or worse. And this was definitely worse.

In fact, this feeling of fear was exactly why she'd stopped taking risks, why she'd chosen Kyle, who was safe and predictable and not the love of her life. Subconsciously she'd known that he would never break her heart the way her father had done with his crimes or the way her mother had done when she'd taken her own life.

But sometime during the night she'd let down her guard and John had walked into her heart. He had to be all right. Someone that young and vibrant, who lived life with such joy, needed many more years – and not just years to exist, but years to live. She couldn't imagine him being damaged. But it was a risk – one he'd taken because of her, he'd said. She'd had no idea when she'd told him about her mother's suicide that he'd been contemplating the same thing. She was glad he'd changed his mind. Now, she just really needed him to wake up and be normal and healthy.

She spent the next two hours leafing through magazines and watching people come in and out of the waiting room. When she was nearing the three-hour mark, Peggy entered the room with two coffees.

"Thought you could use one," she said. "I'm taking a break."

"Thanks." She took a sip of the strong, hot coffee and felt a little better. She hadn't slept much the night before and the waiting and worrying were exhausting.

"So you said you met Eric last night," Peggy said. "How did that happen?"

"We just ran into each other and started talking."

"He's a good-looking guy."

"Yes, and smart, sexy, funny."

"Wow, you've fallen hard." Peggy shook her head. "I've been wanting for you to meet someone since Kyle bailed on you, but did it have to be a guy with a brain tumor?"

"I didn't know he was sick. He took me dancing. He didn't miss a beat."

"You went *dancing*?"

"I know. It was very unlike me. Everything about last night was unlike me. But it was amazing. I tried so hard to be with Kyle, to make that relationship work, to be part of the group."

"What are you talking about? You never needed Kyle to be part of the group."

"It was more comfortable when I wasn't alone. Not that you guys ever tried to make me feel bad when I was on my own, but it wasn't easy to be the only single person in the room."

"I'm so sorry you ever felt that way."

"It was me – not you guys. I was just insecure. But being with John last night changed me. He showed me a side of myself I hadn't seen in a while. I don't want to go back to the safe, boring person I'd become."

"Then don't. Just be you, Liz, whoever that is. I know I'll love her."

"Thanks." She glanced up at the clock. "They should be almost done, right?"

"I think so."

"He has to be all right."

Peggy gave her a commiserating smile. "I'll let you know as soon as they're done."

After Peggy left, Liz leaned her head against the wall and closed her eyes. She didn't know when she drifted off, but suddenly Peggy was shaking her shoulder and offering her a bright smile.

"What happened?" she asked.

"He made it. Dr. Reston said they believe they got all of the tumor and that he'll recover fully."

She put a hand to her mouth, her heart

overflowing with emotion. Tears welled up in her eyes. She'd spent the last decade believing that the worst would always happen, but today she'd been handed a miracle.

"Are you all right?" Peggy asked.

She smiled through her tears. "Happy tears."

"Good. He's going to be out for a while, you know."

"I know."

"When he's better, I want you to bring him over to the house. I need to get to know this guy who's stolen your heart."

"I will if he wants to come. I know how I feel about him. I'm not completely sure how he feels about me, but it doesn't matter. Because the real gift he gave me is the ability to love wholeheartedly again. I'll always be grateful." She took a breath. "I do need to run one errand."

"Go. You have plenty of time before he regains consciousness."

"I'll see you later." She gave Peggy an impulsive hug. "I love you, too, you know." And then she headed out the door.

Faith's Fancies was a small bakery a few miles away. There was a line of people ahead of her, but this time Liz didn't mind waiting. Knowing that John was going to be okay had brightened her whole day. When she finally reached the counter, she said that someone had left a cake for her and gave her name.

A few minutes later, she was handed a small chocolate cake in a pink box. The icing was decorated with a multitude of stars, just like the ones that had sparkled above them all night long. And in the center of the cake were the words: *Love is worth the risk.*

"Yes, it is," she murmured to herself.

She took the cake back to the hospital. John was back in his room but still asleep. She took a seat in the chair by his side, and then she reached for his hand. She'd finally found someone worth keeping, and she didn't intend to let him go.

Epilogue

A year later…

The cake in front of Liz was a rich dark chocolate, much like the one she'd picked up from Faith's Fancies on the day after her last birthday. She couldn't believe it was a coincidence. Smiling across the table at John, she said, "You did this."

"We started a tradition."

They'd started more than that. They'd started a life together, a life filled with love and joy and adventure. The waiters at De Marco's gathered around the table, and as one lit the birthday candle on her cake, the others began to sing.

Their song faded into the background. All she could see was the flickering flame, beckoning to her to make a wish, to trust in fate. But she'd already gotten last year's wish… *someone to love*. Better yet, she'd found someone to love her. "I have nothing left to wish for," she told John.

"There must be something you want."

The waiters finished singing and the crowd in the restaurant broke into applause. She sucked in a big breath, closed her eyes and wished for... *a love that lasts forever*. Then she blew out the candle.

"Do you think you'll get your wish?" John asked when they were alone again.

"I think so," she said confidently. "I felt greedy wishing for anything. We already have so much. You're well now. We're together, and that's all I need."

"Really?" He pulled out a small black velvet box. "What about this?"

She caught her breath at the beautiful, sparkling diamond ring. "Oh, John."

"Will you marry me, Liz?"

"Of course I will," she said without hesitation. The past year had taught her that every day was a risk, but love made it all worthwhile.

He slid the ring on her finger and leaned across the table to kiss her. "I'm the luckiest man in the world."

"I'm the luckiest woman."

"So when can we tie the knot?"

"Whenever you want," she replied. She took a breath. "But if you don't mind waiting a few weeks, I think I'd like to do it when my dad gets out of prison. I'd like him to be there. Not to walk me down the aisle, because he doesn't deserve that privilege. And I don't need him to give me away. I'd just like him to be there. I can give myself away."

John nodded. He knew first-hand how difficult it had been for her to reconnect with her dad. But after John's brush with death, she'd realized that she couldn't let that piece of her life go unsettled. So she'd made the trip to the jail, and she'd seen her father for the first time in ten years. Since then they'd exchanged some letters, and she'd made a couple more visits. They tried to focus on the good memories and not the bad, and slowly she was beginning to get past all the pain.

"I'm proud of you," John said. "You faced your fears."

"How could I not? You showed me the way when you elected to have your surgery."

"I couldn't give up on my life after meeting you."

"I never thought I could fall in love so fast."

"When it's right, it's right."

She glanced across the room as the waiters began another birthday song. "Someone else has my birthday." She blinked as the woman's face came into view. "Hey, I know her. It's the woman from the hotel, the one whose party we crashed."

"I think you're right," John said.

"Her cake is a lot smaller though, and I don't see her husband. But she looks happier now." She paused. "Funny that she should be here. It doesn't feel like a coincidence."

He shrugged. "I'm not going to question fate anymore. After all it brought me you,"

John said as he leaned in for another kiss.

* * *

Carole glanced around the table with a pleased smile. This birthday party was perfect. She had her mother and her kids this year. No big hotel-ballroom party with strangers, just a small dinner with the people she loved the most.

"Make a wish," Nora said, as the waiters finished the obligatory birthday song.

She stared down at the sheet cake, realizing it was a little nicer than the usual free slice that came with a birthday dinner. "This is amazing," she said, noting the decorative night skyline of San Francisco. "Did you do this, Mom?"

"Not me," Nora said with a secretive smile.

She glanced at her daughter and son. Both were grinning from ear to ear. Her relationship with her children had blossomed in the last year, especially since the divorce, which had become official just a week earlier.

She'd tried to get Blake into counseling after her last birthday, but he'd stalled, and after two months of fighting over how their lives were going to go, she'd filed for divorce. It hadn't been an easy decision to make. She'd been his wife since she was twenty-two years old. She hadn't worked during their marriage, except as his corporate wife, so she'd been faced with some scary choices. And Blake had not gone away easily. He'd made her pay dearly for her decision. She hadn't realized how much of his money he'd hidden away until it had come time to settle their divorce. But in the end, the money hadn't mattered. She'd needed her freedom. And with that freedom had come a new relationship with her children.

They'd handled the divorce better than expected, not even complaining when she'd moved them into a smaller house. Because what they'd given up in acreage, they'd gotten back in love. She'd become a part of their lives. It hadn't happened overnight, but every day they grew closer, and she would never regret her decision to put them before her marriage. They'd been worth the fight.

"Did you two do this?" she asked.

"It wasn't us," Sophie said. "But someone who knows you really well said he owed you a cake. So we let him get you this one."

"Alex," she said with a soft smile. She'd introduced Alex to her kids a month ago. At first, they'd been wary of another man coming into their lives, but Alex had won them over. He was good with them. He respected them, and he didn't try to act like a father figure. He was just their friend.

Her relationship with Alex had evolved slowly. It had taken her months to get him to trust her enough to have dinner with her. He hadn't wanted to be her rebound guy, or the one she ran back to just because she was lonely. She'd had to prove to him she could stand on her own and that she knew what she wanted – who she wanted. She'd appreciated the time, because she'd needed to prove that to herself, too. She'd used her experience planning her husband's parties to get a part-time job with a local wedding consultant, and found the work and the new friendships to be just what she needed to heal. Life was good now.

"Looks like I'm just in time," Alex said, appearing at the table. "I know you wanted just family tonight," he added, "But Nora and the kids thought you might not mind if I showed up for cake."

"I don't mind at all. It's a beautiful cake. It reminds me of the view from the park."

"The one you used to dream on," he said, meeting her gaze. "You'd better make your wish before the candle burns all the way down.

She closed her eyes and smiled. Last year she'd wanted…*her family back*. And that wish had come true. So this year…*Love and joy and happiness for all of us*.

She opened her eyes and blew out the candle.

"What did you wish for?" Sophie asked.

"It's a secret. She can't tell you, or it won't come true," Nora interjected.

"Please," Sophie begged.

"Maybe she wished for you to stop talking," Michael said.

Sophie punched her brother in the arm. "Maybe she wished for you to disappear."

"She wouldn't do that. She likes me better than you."

"She does not," Sophie countered.

Carole smiled at their bickering. She didn't mind their arguments, because she was a part of them. They were no longer eating with the nanny in the other room as they'd done so often when they were growing up.

"Why don't you sit down, Alex?" she suggested. "We can make room."

As Alex squeezed into the booth next to her, they were all touching shoulder to shoulder. "My life is so good," she said. "I thought forty was the end, but it turns out it was just the beginning." She lifted her glass. "To us."

"To us," they echoed, clinking glasses.

As they finished the toast, the waiters gathered around the table next to hers and once again burst into song.

"You've got competition," Alex said.

She stared at the brunette woman sitting at the next table and realized with amazement that she'd seen her before – a year ago to the day. The moment flashed in her head. After seeing Blake with Krystal, she'd run out of the hotel and into the street, right in front of a car. *That woman's car.* She'd almost been run over. It was then that she'd realized how close she'd come to dying. It was then that she'd realized she'd been given a second chance. How odd that they shared the same birthday. And yet it was strangely fitting, too.

* * *

Angela blushed as the waiters sang long and loud. It was certainly a busy birthday night in the restaurant. "I told you not to say it was my birthday, Colin."

Her husband shrugged. "Hey, I got you out of the big family party this year. Your mother may never speak to me again."

"She'll survive. And we're going to see her tomorrow anyway."

"Can I help you blow out the candles?" Kimmie asked, getting on her knees on the bench seat next to Angela.

"She has to make her wish first," Laurel said. "Be patient."

She smiled at Kimmie and Laurel, thinking how much they'd grown in the past year and how much they'd changed. After that first night in her apartment, the girls had spent several weeks in two separate foster homes despite her pleas to keep them together. Knowing the girls were apart, she and Colin had worked harder and faster to be licensed as foster parents. Eventually Laurel and Kimmie had been placed in their care while their mother went through rehab.

For months they'd all hoped that the girls' mother would recover enough to take care of them, but every rehab stint ended in failure. In a heartbreaking moment of motherly love, Laurel's mother had finally admitted she couldn't take care of them. After seeing how happy her girls were, she'd agreed to give up her parental rights.

Now Angela and Colin were making plans to officially adopt the girls. They were going to be a family. It seemed shocking that it had all started when Laurel had tried to mug her.

"What are you smiling at?" Colin asked.

"Just thinking about how we all met."

Laurel flushed. "I thought we weren't going to talk about it ever again. I did a stupid thing that night."

"It was stupid, but I think it was also fate," Angela said. "Before I ran into you, I spoke to an old friend. He's a priest now. I told him that I wouldn't come back to church unless I had a child, and he told me that God loves a good challenge. A half hour later, I met you."

"And now we go to church on Sundays," Laurel said with a grin.

"I had to keep up my end of the

bargain," she replied.

"Honey, make your wish," Colin said.

"Last year I wished for a baby," she said. "But I got two beautiful girls instead."

"So what's it going to be this year?" Colin asked.

She gave him a little smile and wished for … *a little boy to make our family complete*. Then she blew out the candle.

"Are you going to tell us your wish?" Laurel asked.

"You'll all find out in about six months."

"What?" Colin asked, confusion and a hint of wonder in his gaze. "What are you talking about, Angie?"

"I'm pregnant, Colin. I don't know how it happened, but I passed the three-month mark yesterday. I didn't want to tell you until I knew whether it was going to take. I didn't want any of us to be disappointed. But it looks like I'm doing okay."

"Are you serious? This is unbelievable."

It was unbelievable. They hadn't done the IVF, because they'd spent their money on the girls.

"The doctor said it wasn't completely uncommon for women to conceive after they gave up worrying about getting pregnant. Something about relaxing," she said.

"I can't believe it," Colin said again.

"You're going to have a baby?" Laurel asked, a worried gleam in her eyes.

"A little brother or sister for you and Kimmie," she said. "Colin and I are still adopting you. We already consider you both our daughters, and our lives have been incredibly blessed by your presence. Now we're going to welcome one more."

"I always thought three kids was the perfect number," Colin said.

"I want a little brother," Kimmie said.

"Me, too," Laurel added.

"Boy or girl, our child will be loved," Angela said. She watched as Colin cut the cake. "It's been another great birthday. I didn't think I could top last year, but every year gets better and better." As she looked around the restaurant, she saw two other cakes, two other women who were celebrating their birthdays. "Oh, my God," she said, sitting up straight. "Those women…"

"What women?" Colin asked.

"The other two women celebrating their birthdays tonight. I met both of them last year on my birthday. The brunette with the guy – she was in the drugstore when I went to buy Kimmie cough medicine. She had condoms and said she was hoping to get lucky."

"Looks like that worked out," Colin said dryly.

"And the blonde over there – I almost ran her down with the car when I first left our house. I was so angry and hurt that I couldn't see straight. And she was running away from someone. I remember she jumped into a limo and took off. I had no idea we all shared the same birthday. It's strange that we'd end up here a year later."

"Fate," Colin said. "And everyone looks happy."

She couldn't agree more, because the other two women were both looking back at her with wide smiles on their faces and sparks of recognition. "I have a feeling all our wishes came true," she said.

"Guess you were born on a lucky day."

"We all were."

THE END

Continue reading for an excerpt from JUST
A WISH AWAY, Book #2 in The Wish
Series...

EXCERPT
JUST A WISH AWAY
@ 2012 Barbara Freethy

Prologue

Fifteen years earlier …

"Race you to Dragon Rock," Braden Elliott challenged.

Twelve-year-old Alexa Parker barely heard him. Her attention was focused on the pile of pebbles and shells that had washed ashore. She was looking for tiny shards of sea glass or mermaid tears, as the locals called them. The Sand Harbor Beach on the coast of Washington State was known for the glass that the sea tossed up after years of being tumbled and turned by the waves and the salt water, finally landing on the sand as beautiful, colorful gems. When she grew up, she wanted to become a glassmaker, turn all those broken pieces into something amazing.

"Come on, Alexa," Braden urged.

She looked up at him, her determination wavering as she stared into his beautiful green eyes, that sometimes reminded her of the glass she collected. Braden had grown three inches over the summer, now towering over her at nearly six feet. His brown hair was thick and wavy and messed up by the wind. He was so cute; sometimes she just couldn't stop looking at him.

They'd known each other since they were ten, but this was the first summer she'd looked at him as more than just a friend. In fact, her stomach did a little flip flop every time he smiled at her. She didn't really know what to do about her new feelings. Part of her wanted to say something and the other part of her was just too scared. A couple of her friends had boyfriends, but she wasn't sure she was ready, and she only saw Braden in the summer.

While Braden lived at Sand Harbor year round, she only came for holidays and summers. Every June, she and her mom packed up the car and left Seattle to stay with her Aunt Phoebe at the beach. Her dad would come down on Thursdays and take long weekends in July and August. It was the perfect way to spend the summer.

She'd met some of Braden's Sand Harbor friends over the years, but when she was in town it was mostly just the two of them. They would meet up every morning on their bikes and take off to explore one of the three beaches that dotted the coastline. They'd search for sea glass, fly kites, build sand castles and make up stories about the people who vacationed in the big houses along the bluff. Sand Harbor was a quiet fishing village in the winter, but in summer, the town filled up with tourists and celebrities looking for a summer escape. Every year there seemed to be new houses being built along the bluffs.

"Alexa," Braden said impatiently. "You're daydreaming again."

It was a bad habit of hers, but one that didn't usually make him mad. Braden put his hands in the pockets of his jeans and stared out to sea, and she realized Braden's bad mood was more about his dad than about her. Braden's father was a soldier in the Army, and he was supposed to have come home by now, but they kept postponing his release date. Now they were talking about Christmas. Braden seemed to grow more worried with each passing day, and she knew that deep down he was afraid that his dad would never come home.

Wanting to cheer him up, she got to her feet. "Okay, I'll race you," she said. Making Braden smile again seemed more important than finding glass to add to her collection.

Her words did make him smile and no wonder. Braden loved action, running, biking, hiking. He hated to stand still.

She tossed the few pieces of glass she had collected into her backpack.

"I'll carry it for you," Braden said, taking the pack out of her hands. "I don't want you to say the backpack slowed you down."

"Fine." Braden would beat her whether she was carrying anything or not. She couldn't keep up with his long legs.

"And I'll give you a head start," he added.

She didn't bother to say thanks, just took off down the beach. She didn't like to run as much as Braden did, but there were times like this afternoon when it felt good to have the wind in her hair and the sun on her face. She was going to miss summer, and she was going to miss Braden.

Moisture filled her eyes. She hadn't told him yet about the change in plans. She hadn't wanted to ruin the day, but as the sun sank down to meet the sea she knew she was almost out of time.

Braden passed her, his stride long and easy, as if he wasn't making any effort at all, and he probably wasn't. He was a born athlete.

By the time she got to the rock that looked like a dragon, Braden was sprawled on the sand, a satisfied smile on his face.

She flopped down, breathless, her cheeks warm from the sun and the run.

Braden gazed at her with an odd expression in his eyes. Her heart skipped a beat.

He looked like he wanted to kiss her.

Surprise and nervousness flared. She'd never kissed a boy, but she wanted to kiss Braden. She just didn't know how to get from where she was to where he was. There had to be at least three feet between them.

"You're staring at me," she said, licking her suddenly dry lips.

"You're – pretty."

Her heart skipped another beat. "I am?"

"You know you are." His jaw tightened, and then he jumped to his feet. "Hey, what's that?" He took off, jogging toward the base of the cliff.

She got up more slowly, disappointed that nothing had happened. Her friend at home, Colette, had already kissed two boys. Braden had said she was pretty, but maybe she wasn't pretty enough. She always freckled in the summer, and her fair skin was more likely to burn than tan. Her blonde hair was pulled back in a ponytail, because it tangled so easily in the wind. It certainly wasn't thin and silky like Colette's. And she didn't have on any make up, because her mother wouldn't let her wear more than lip gloss, even though she was in middle school.

No wonder Braden hadn't kissed her. He was one of the most popular boys in Sand Harbor. There were always girls calling out to him when they rode into town. She'd always felt a little special that she was the one he was with. But maybe that's because she liked to explore and was more of a tomboy.

"Alexa, come on," Braden said impatiently.

She walked over to join him. "What?"

"Look." He pulled out a sparkly, oddly shaped blue glass bottle from the sand. They'd found bottles before, but nothing like this. It appeared very old and unusual, like it had come from a shipwreck. "Wow," she murmured, dropping to her knees beside him. She took the bottle from him and spun it around, the blue turning to purple and red in the dusky light. "It's beautiful."

"You could break it apart and mix it with your other glass and make something amazing."

"Oh, no, I couldn't break this apart. Look at the colors. They're -- magical."

"Magic doesn't exist."

"It does if you believe."

"Well, I don't believe."

"Why not?"

"Because I don't," he said with a frown. "It's stupid. Magic is just about tricks."

"Not real magic," she argued. "Not miracle kind of magic."

He rolled his eyes.

"This could be a genie's bottle," she said, her imagination taking hold as she spun the glass in her hands. The colors created a kaleidoscope, a fast-moving rainbow, unlike anything she'd ever seen. She glanced over at Braden, who still had an expression of disgust on his face, but behind that stubborn glint in his eye was a hint of hope. And she fed on that hope. "If we pull out the cork, a genie might appear, and then we'll get to make a wish," she said.

"Yeah, right."

"You should try to believe."

"Why?"

"Because if you don't try, it might not work. And I want to make a wish. It's important to me."

"It's just a bottle, Alexa. It doesn't matter if you make a wish or not, because it won't come true."

She ignored him, her fingers tightening on the cork. There was something so compelling about the bottle that she couldn't believe it was something ordinary. There was no label on it, nothing to suggest what had once been inside, or might still be inside. It felt light, empty, but the glass was so thick, it was impossible to be sure. So she pulled the cork. It didn't budge. She tried again, but she couldn't move it.

"Give me that," Braden said. He grabbed the bottle and yanked out the cork.

As he did so, a spray of water hit her right in the face. She gasped at the unexpected wave that had hit the beach so close to them. They were yards away from where the tide usually hit. Wiping the salt water from her eyes, she stared at Braden. "What was that?"

"Just a wave," he said, running a hand through his damp hair. But there was an odd look in his eyes.

The air around them was suddenly misty. Where had the fog come from? Just minutes ago it had been sunny. She shivered, as the bottle seemed to glow between them. She waited for some figure to appear, but nothing happened.

"There's no genie," Braden said, an unexpected note of disappointment in his voice.

She took the bottle out of his hands. The glass was warmer than it had been. "Let's wish anyway," she said, feeling as if it were suddenly very important.

"Alexa –"

"Please, Braden. You have to put your hand on the bottle, too."

"I still think this is stupid."

"I understand. But do it anyway."

After a brief hesitation, he put his hand on the bottle, his fingers covering hers.

She didn't know if the magic was in the bottle or in his touch, but she felt hot all over.

Closing her eyes, she thought for a moment, and then silently whispered...

"I wish Braden would fall in love with me."

The wish scared her a little. She didn't really understand love. She just knew she wanted to feel it. And she wanted Braden to feel it, too.

Opening her eyes, she caught Braden gazing back at her. She hoped he couldn't see the wish in her eyes. She'd feel so dumb. "What did you wish for?" she asked.

"I can't tell you."

"We tell each other everything," she protested.

"Not wishes," he said.

"Did you really make one?" she asked suspiciously.

He grinned. "That's for me to know and you to find out."

"Sometimes, I hate you," she said, hoping he'd never guess what her wish was.

With the fog hitting the beach, the sky had grown very dark. It was getting late, and she had no more time in which to stall.

"I have to tell you something," she said.

"What's that?"

"We're leaving tomorrow."

His jaw dropped and a frown turned down his lips. "Summer isn't over for two more weeks."

"I know, but my mom says we have to go."

"Why?"

"My parents aren't getting along."

"What else is new?" he asked. "They never get along."

"Well, it's worse now. They got into a huge fight last night. My dad slammed out of the house, and he didn't come home until this morning. He barely said anything to anyone, just packed up his stuff and left. My mom says we have to go back to Seattle so she can talk to him."

"Why doesn't she go by herself?"

"She said it's almost the end of summer anyway. I told her I wanted to stay, Braden, but she wouldn't listen. She was crying all night. I could hear her from my room after I went to bed. She's so angry and so sad."

"That sucks."

She let out a sigh. "Yeah, it does."

He stared at her for a long minute, his expression unreadable. "When are you coming back?"

"We usually come at Thanksgiving." Her stomach twisted into a knot as she realized how far away that was. She'd never worried before about Braden not being there when she came back for visits, but they were growing up, and it wouldn't be long before he got a girlfriend. He'd pick someone in town, someone who wasn't always leaving. And then where would she be?

"Thanksgiving, huh? That's not for months," he said heavily.

"I know. But we'll call and write, right?"

"Sure."

He didn't sound very convincing and lately she hadn't been able to read him as well as she used to.

"I guess we should go," she said. She wished she could make this day last forever, because she had a terrible fear that she might never see Braden again, that after today everything would change – unless her wish came true. She really needed a little magic right now. Everything else in her life was turning so dark.

As they walked across the sand, she told herself to stop getting so worked up. She would see Braden again. They were coming back in November. It was only a couple of months. But her mental pep talk did little to ease the tension in her body and the worry in her mind.

The lights were coming on in the houses above them, some casting long shadows on the sand, giving an eerie, almost surreal quality to the dusky evening. The big castle-like house that was one of her favorites was just in front of them, and she couldn't help looking up at the widow's walk, wondering if she would see the beautiful woman with the long red hair who often stood on the deck in a swirling white gown that made her seem almost like a ghost. She'd nicknamed her Ariel, because she reminded her of a mermaid.

Her heart skipped a beat as she saw the woman, but Ariel was definitely more alive than ghostly right now. She was shouting at someone – someone in the shadows.

Braden paused, too, his gaze moving upward.

"You lied to me," the woman shouted, her voice frenzied and filled with the pain of some betrayal.

Alexa couldn't hear what the other person said, but it did nothing to calm Ariel. She picked up something and threw it into the shadows. At the sound of a crash, Alexa moved a little closer to Braden, unsettled by the fight. While her parents hadn't resorted to throwing things at each other, they fought with the same kind of intense anger. She didn't understand how people could go from loving each other to hating each other.

"Don't tell me to be quiet," the woman yelled. "I'm tired of secrets. I can't keep it all in. I'm going to snap." She paused. "Don't touch me. I'll come in when I want to come in."

"We should go," Alexa said, her stomach feeling a little sick.

"Looks like she went inside anyway," Braden observed. "I wonder who she was arguing with and what all the secrets are about."

Normally, Alexa loved secrets, but not today. "I don't care. I just wish everyone would stop fighting. I hate when people yell at each other. It makes me feel sick to my stomach. How does love turn into hate?"

"It's going to be okay, Alexa."

"I wish I could believe that," she said as they started walking again.

"If you can believe in magic, you can believe in that," he said.

She sighed. "Maybe you're right. Maybe there is no magic."

He shook his head. "No, I don't want you to think that. I need you to believe."

"Why?" she asked, giving him a curious look.

His lips tightened and then he said, "Because then I can try to believe."

She gazed into his eyes and saw a need she could fulfill. "Then I will."

He nodded and they walked the rest of the way in silence.

When they reached their bikes, Braden handed over her backpack, and she put the genie's bottle inside.

"Do you want me to carry the backpack while you ride?" Braden offered.

"No, I can hang on to it," she said, slipping the straps over her shoulder. She didn't want to let go of the bottle, because when she got home, she was going to make another wish, a wish that her parents would stop fighting. It had occurred to her that she might have wasted her wish on her own chance at love, when what she should have been concentrating on was getting her parents back on the same page.

"Alexa," Braden said as she got on her bike.

"Yes?" she asked.

He moved his bike next to hers, then leaned over and kissed her on the mouth. His lips were firm and warm, a little salty, but actually quite perfect.

Before she could really register the fact that she'd just gotten her first kiss, he pulled away.

His voice was a little gruff when he said, "Come back, Alexa, okay?"

"I will," she promised, her heart racing.

Then she got on her bike and followed him down the road, wondering how long it would be before she saw him again.

Chapter One

Present Day …

When Alexa Parker was twelve years old, two monumental events happened. She fell in love for the very first time, and her parents got divorced. Alexa couldn't think of one event without the other. Now, returning to Sand Harbor as a twenty-seven-year-old adult, she was reminded of both.

Every street in the picturesque beach town seemed to hold a memory, the rocky path to the beach that she and Braden had ridden their bikes down every day, the Boardwalk with the cotton candy and hot pretzel carts that were crowded with kids in the summer, the fishing boats coming into the harbor after a long day at sea, Nini's Pancake House, where her dad used to take her on Sunday mornings, and the majestic houses on the bluffs that she'd dreamed about one day living in.

Like so many of her childhood dreams, living in a big house on her favorite beach was one that had fallen by the wayside. The same was true for her dream of becoming a glassmaker, of turning beautiful pieces of sea glass into something amazing, and also her dream of marrying her best friend. But those had been the dreams of an idealistic girl, who'd thought everything in life would always be perfect, exactly like that perfect summer kiss from Braden the very last time she'd seen him.

She was a different person now. She could barely remember that naïve girl, but she'd never forgotten her first kiss.

Unfortunately, her relationship with Braden had not lasted past that summer. Her parents' divorce had changed her life in every possible way. She and her mom had moved back East, far away from the Washington coast. Her dad had ended up in Los Angeles a few years later and had remarried and had other children.

The first few years she'd tried to keep in touch with Braden, but she'd had her hands full dealing with her mom's extreme depression and the move to a new city and a new school. Sand Harbor had seemed very far away. Their contact had faded to occasional calls and emails and then eventually nothing.

Braden had had his own problems to deal with, including the death of his father, who'd been killed in action when Braden was fifteen. She'd tried to get in touch with him then, but he'd never called her back. Her mother said she couldn't afford to fly her across the country for the funeral. That was pretty much the end of their tenuous relationship.

Years passed, and she dated other guys, but she was never quite able to get Braden out of her mind. Thinking she'd give it one more shot, she'd gone to Sand Harbor right after her college graduation. She was too late. She was shocked to learn that Braden had married at twenty, just weeks before enlisting in the Army.

The dream of her heart was finally shut down. Braden was taken. He was with someone else. She had to move on with her life.

That had been six years ago.

Now she was back in Sand Harbor, and she had no idea where Braden was, but it didn't matter. She wasn't here for Braden, she was here for her aunt, Phoebe Gray, who had been injured in a break-in at her antique store. While Alexa had been kept away from everyone connected to her father's side of the family, she had reunited with her father's older sister, Phoebe, on her last visit to Sand Harbor.

They'd been in frequent contact since then, a fact she'd happily kept from her mother, who was still quite bitter about that side of the family. But Alexa didn't blame her aunt or her uncle or her cousins for her parents' divorce. And she'd enjoyed getting to know them again over the past few years. Most of the contact was over email or through online social sites, but it was a start. When her cousin, Evie, had called her at dawn to tell her about the robbery, she'd immediately said she was on her way. She hadn't always been there for her aunt, but she could be there now.

She'd caught the first plane out of San Francisco, rented a car, and made the two-hour drive from Seattle to Sand Harbor. She'd stopped at the hospital first, but her aunt was unconscious, and the doctor said it could be hours before she woke up. Several of Phoebe's friends were in the waiting room, so reassured that her aunt would not be alone when she woke up, Alexa had decided to track down Evie and see what was happening with the police investigation.

Pulling into a spot down the street from her aunt's antique shop, aptly named Yesterday Once More, she drew in a deep breath and then stepped out of the car. The store was one of many boutiques on a downtown side street. Although, there were some foot traffic, there weren't quite as many tourists on this block. The shop sat between a vintage clothing store and a beauty salon. A small walkway separated the antique shop from the salon; a path many used to cut through to the main post office on the next block.

As Alexa approached the shop, she was again assailed with memories. Her aunt had opened Yesterday Once More thirty years ago, and almost everyone in the family had worked there at some time or another, herself included. She'd loved helping out in the store on her summer vacations. Like her aunt, she was captivated by anything that was old and came with a story. Imagining where the pieces had come from and who had used them had been one of her favorite pastimes.

Her gut tightened as she reached the shop. The big bay window was intact, but the glass over the front door had been shattered and was now boarded up with wood. Remnants of yellow crime scene tape clung to the frame. She still couldn't believe someone had broken into the shop. There had not been a lot of crime in Sand Harbor when she was growing up, but perhaps things had changed.

Seeing someone inside the shop, she tried the doorknob, but it was locked, so she knocked. A moment later, a woman's face peered around the corner of a large desk in the front window. Alexa waved, recognizing her cousin's dark brown hair and pretty blue eyes. Evie was the oldest daughter of her father's brother, Stan.

"Alexa," Evie, said with a relieved smile, as she opened the door. "I'm so glad you came."

Alexa gave Evie a hug and then glanced around the crowded showroom. Her aunt had always had plenty of inventory, but she'd also been very disciplined about keeping her displays organized. Now, everything was in chaos. Smaller items were strewn across the floor and on some of the tables and desks. There was broken glass as well as shattered tiles and ceramics on the floor. It looked as if the thief had been more interested in destroying the pieces rather than stealing them, but that didn't make sense.

"Wow," she murmured. "I had no idea it would be this bad."

Evie nodded, her lips drawing together in a tense line. "It's horrible."

"Have the police caught the person or people who did this?"

"Not yet. The Chief of Police, Edwin Hayes, actually found Aunt Phoebe. They're good friends, and he said he'd had a hunch she might be working late, so he'd stopped by. If he hadn't done so, it might have been morning before anyone found her. She'd already lost a lot of blood by the time the paramedics got there.

Alexa followed her cousin's gaze to the dark red stain on the floor by the front counter. Her stomach turned over as she realized how close her aunt had come to losing her life.

"They don't know if Aunt Phoebe was struck from behind or if she hit her head on the counter when she fell, but she has a big gash on the back of her head," Evie added.

"I saw the bandage around her head. I stopped by the hospital on my way here. She was asleep and surrounded by friends. I thought I might be of more help if I came here."

Evie nodded. "That makes sense. I'm going to stop by this evening. Aunt Phoebe's friend, Louise, promised to call me if there's any change." Evie paused. "I feel so bad about what happened. It's partly my fault."

"Why would you say that?" Alexa asked in surprise.

"I came by here yesterday afternoon. Aunt Phoebe had just gotten in a big delivery from the Wellbourne estate, all those boxes," she added, pointing to a stack of eight to ten boxes, some of which were opened and upturned on the floor, some of which were still sealed. "She told me she was going to come back after dinner and get a head start on unpacking, because the weekends are so busy and she wanted to make room in the store before the tourists descended."

"You couldn't have predicted a robbery, Evie."

"No, but I knew she was going to be in

the store late at night. I should have tried to dissuade her from coming in alone or persuaded her to wait until today. I also could have offered to help. Beverly Adams, Aunt Phoebe's assistant, is on vacation until next week."

"Evie, stop it. Aunt Phoebe wouldn't have been persuaded to wait even if you'd tried to talk her into it. This shop is her baby and she watches over it like a hawk. Besides that, she's stubborn."

"Stubbornness is a Parker family trait," Evie said with a sigh.

"Exactly."

"I'm so glad you were able to come, Alexa. My parents are in Europe right now, and I haven't been able to catch up with them yet, so I want to make sure I'm taking care of everything."

"I'll help you however I can." Alexa said.

"I appreciate that. Did you speak to your parents? Is your father coming?"

"I left a message for my dad, but he hasn't returned my call. That's not unusual. We don't talk often, especially since his wife had another baby."

"I can't believe your father is having babies at his age," Evie said, raising an eyebrow.

"His wife is fourteen years younger," she said, deliberately keeping her tone neutral. She didn't want to get into her feelings about her dad's marriage. She should have been used to it all by now. It had been twelve years since he'd married his second wife, and this new baby was number four.

"And your mom?" Evie asked somewhat tentatively.

"She's actually the best I've seen her in years. She got remarried last year, and her husband is in the wine business. She often goes on trips with him, and she seems happy."

"I'm glad for her and for you."

"Thanks."

"Aunt Phoebe will be happy to see you when she wakes up."

Alexa liked the hopeful note in Evie's voice. She didn't want to think about the possibility that her aunt would never wake up. That was too awful to contemplate. "So what can I do?" she asked.

"If you want to start with clean up, that would be great. I have to pick up my twins from school in a few minutes, so I won't be able to do much more today. If you unpack anything, just make sure to write down each item with a brief description. Aunt Phoebe is a stickler for details."

"I remember that from when I worked here as a kid."

"Some things don't change," Evie said

with a smile.

"So the shipment is from an estate?"

"The Wellbournes. They own that big house on the bluff."

"Oh, sure," she said. That house had served as the foundation for many a daydream, not only because it was enormous, but also because there had always been an air of mystery about it. She and Braden had made up numerous stories about the people who had stayed there.

"Jack Wellbourne died last week, and left some of his antiques to Aunt Phoebe."

"That was nice of him."

"She was very excited to see what he'd left her. Apparently, he was quite a collector." Evie grabbed some keys off the counter and tossed them to her. "Lock up when you leave. In fact, you might want to keep the door locked until we're sure there won't be any more trouble." She paused. "If you'd rather not be here alone, we can leave this for later."

That was a tempting thought, but Alexa knew that her aunt would want the shop put back in order as soon as possible, and she had nothing else to do. It was broad daylight, and there were a number of people on the street, so she didn't feel in any danger.

"I don't mind cleaning up and getting some pieces inventoried," she said. "I might as well do something productive."

"If it makes you feel better, the police said they'd keep an eye on the shop for the next few days."

"That's good."

"Where are you staying?"

"I reserved a room at the Cheshire Inn."

"You could have stayed with us. Although, twin six-year-olds, two dogs and a cat make life a little hectic."

"But you're happy," Alexa said, seeing the sparkle of pride and love in Evie's eyes when she talked about her family.

"I am stressed a lot of the time, but life is still pretty wonderful." Her gaze softened. "It's good to have you here, Alexa. I hate what happened to our family. One minute we were all spending awesome summers and holidays together, and then you and your parents were gone. I missed you."

"I missed you, too."

"Did you miss anyone else? Like Braden Elliott?" Evie asked with a mischievous sparkle in her eye.

"Braden was my friend a long time ago."

"You two were inseparable that last summer you were here." Evie paused. "He's back, you know."

Her heart jumped. "Really? I thought he was serving overseas."

"He was until three months ago. Aunt

Phoebe didn't tell you?"

"No, but I've been busy with tax season. We haven't been emailing lately." She cleared her throat. "Is Braden still in the Army?"

"I think he's done. He was injured in action several months ago. I don't know the details, but he was in a hospital for about two weeks before he came back here. I've only seen him once from a distance, and at the time he was using a cane. That was awhile ago."

Her throat tightened at the thought of Braden being hurt. "I'm sorry to hear that, but he has a wife to help him get through it."

Evie shook her head. "Not anymore. She asked him for a divorce before he was even out of the hospital."

"Are you serious? How could she do that to her injured husband?"

"She's a bitch from what I hear. I don't know her. But most people think she's pretty hard-hearted. Anyway, Braden rented an apartment and has been keeping to himself since he got home." She paused. "Maybe you should go by and see him."

"I don't think so," she said quickly.

"Why not?"

It was a good question. And the real answer was because she was scared. But she couldn't begin to explain her muddled thoughts to Evie. So she said, "Because we don't know each other anymore. I'm sure I'm the last person he wants to see right now. Braden is part of my past. He was a childhood crush, that's all. There's nothing between us now."

Evie shrugged and gave her a small smile. "Not yet anyway."

* * *

"You need to work, Braden. And I could use your help."

Braden rocked the wooden chair in his kitchen back on two legs, folded his arms across his chest, ignored the ache in his healing ribs and stared across the table at his longtime friend, Drew Lassen. Drew had gone from skateboarder to police officer, a path Braden had never foreseen his once wild and rebellious friend taking. But then they'd both changed a lot since their high school days. "I'm not a cop," he said simply. "And I don't need to work. I'm supposed to be resting."

"You've been resting, and you can't sit in this apartment all day every day." Drew glanced around the room, a frown spreading across his face as he took in the bare furnishings. "This place sucks."

"It's fine."

"It's depressing. You should have gone to your mom's house."

He shook his head. "The last thing I need is my mother hovering over me."

"Where's the rest of your stuff?"

"Kinley has it," he said shortly.

"You're being generous to a woman who doesn't deserve it."

"There's nothing she has that I want anymore." As the words left his mouth, he realized just how true they were.

"Fine, but I've known you a long time, and you're not someone who just sits around."

"I'm recuperating, didn't you hear?" he asked, a cynical note in his voice as he remembered all the platitudes he'd been offered by the doctors who'd attended to him in recent months, as if time would heal all his wounds. That simply wasn't possible. Most of his wounds weren't physical.

"You look like you're ready to be back on your feet," Drew said.

"I'm sure you have enough manpower to keep the citizens of Sand Harbor safe," he said.

"Ordinarily yes, but two officers are out sick and another is on vacation. Plus, I need to provide extra security for Daniel Stone's fundraiser on Saturday night. He's launching his senate campaign here in Sand Harbor this weekend."

"Trying to remind the locals he was born here?" Braden asked cynically. Daniel

Stone's parents owned a house in Sand Harbor, but the Stones were very wealthy and had homes all over the world.

"I don't care about his reason, just what it means for me – which is more security."

"I'm sure he can afford to hire his own security."

"Well, I don't need your help with Stone." Drew paused. "Did you hear about the break-in at Phoebe Gray's antique shop?"

"No," he said, his gut tightening at the mention of Alexa's aunt. No matter how many years passed, every time he saw Phoebe or heard something about her, he thought about Alexa.

"It happened last night," Drew said. "I'm surprised no one told you."

"I haven't spoken to anyone." Since he'd returned home, his mother and sister had been driving him crazy, asking him every two seconds how he felt, whether he needed anything. He knew they were concerned, but he needed to be on his own for a while so he could sort out his life.

"Phoebe went down to her store last night and interrupted a robbery. She was knocked out and has a serious concussion."

He was shocked. "I can't believe it. Do you have any leads?"

"None. We've had some vandalism around town, but nothing to this extent, and certainly no one was assaulted in the previous incidents. We're hoping when Phoebe wakes up, she'll be able to give us some information, but until then, I'd like to get your help. You can use some of those investigative skills you acquired in Army Intelligence."

"Did you run this by your boss?" he asked doubtfully.

"I mentioned it to Chief Hayes. I made it clear that you would just be helping out on a peripheral level, and he was fine with it. He's good friends with Phoebe and he doesn't want to leave any stone unturned. He's also aware that we're shorthanded, and you have an excellent background for this kind of work. Plus, you're a local boy. People will talk to you."

"I don't know, Drew."

"Do you have something better to do?" Drew challenged.

"Obviously I don't," he said. "What exactly do you expect me to do?"

"Look around the store, see if we missed anything, ask some questions, talk to the other shop owners."

"I suppose I could do that," he said slowly. He liked Phoebe, and she was Alexa's aunt. He wondered if Alexa had heard about the robbery. He drew in a deep breath, just the thought of her unsettling him. It had been years since he'd let himself think about her for longer than a second. "I'll stop by there tomorrow."

"Go today," Drew said as he got to his feet. "Let me know if you find anything."

* * *

It was six o'clock and the May sky was starting to darken when Braden approached the antique store. He'd always liked twilight -- that in between time between day and night when everything seemed very still. It was a Wednesday evening and most of the shops closed up by five during the week.

He hadn't been in the antique store since he was a kid, probably not since that last summer he'd hung out with Alexa. She used to help her aunt on the weekends and occasionally he joined her, although he'd never been as interested in the antiques as she had been. She'd loved making up stories about the treasures they sold, and like always he'd gotten caught up in her imagination. She could take almost anything and spin it into a story so real he thought it had actually happened. He'd admired her ability to escape reality so easily. Unfortunately, her imagination had been honed by an unhappy home life. She'd told him that when her parents started fighting, she'd pull the covers over her head and make up stories where she was part of some big, happy family.

His household had been much happier, but his father had been gone a lot. He was career Army, and they'd moved around a lot before his mom finally decided to settle in Sand Harbor where her family was. He'd met Alexa shortly after his arrival, and he'd connected with her instantly. The reality that his dad might not make it home had been with him constantly. It was that nagging worry that had made escaping into Alexa's stories even more appealing. They'd been quite a pair, sharing everything. He'd told her things he'd never imagined he'd say out loud, much less to another person.

A pang of nostalgia tightened his throat. Damn! He really didn't need this trip down memory lane. The last couple of months had been brutal, and he wasn't close to being a hundred percent in any part of his life.

But this wasn't about Alexa; it was about her aunt. If he could do anything to help find out who had put Phoebe in the hospital, he was more than happy to help.

There were lights on in the store, and through the front window, he could see someone moving around inside. The boarded-up door told him the break-in had been rough and unsophisticated. Maybe it had been some restless teenagers thinking it might be fun to vandalize the antique shop and hadn't realized anyone would come by after normal work hours.

He turned the knob, but the door was locked. Knocking sharply on the wood, he hoped one of Phoebe's assistants could give him more information about what had happened.

A moment later the door opened a few inches. A woman gave him a wary look. In the shadowy light, he thought his eyes were playing on tricks on him. But as the surprise flared in her blue gaze, his breath stopped.

Alexa!

She pulled the door all the way open, and for a moment all he could do was look at her. She was dressed in dark jeans, black boots, and a coral-colored sweater that hugged her curves. Her blonde hair was swept back from her face in a thick ponytail that hung past her shoulders. There was only a hint of the freckles that had once dotted her nose. Dark lashes framed her beautiful eyes and her light pink lips were soft and sexy.

Damn! She'd been a fantasy in his head for so long he could hardly believe she was real. He needed to catch his breath, find his voice.

But she beat him to it.

"Braden?" she said. "Is it really you?"

END OF EXCERPT

Booklist

<u>The Wish Series</u>
#1 A Secret Wish
#2 Just A Wish Away

<u>Standalone Novels</u>
All She Ever Wanted
Almost Home
Ask Mariah
Daniel's Gift
Don't Say A Word
Golden Lies
Just The Way You Are
Love Will Find A Way
One True Love
Ryan's Return
Some Kind of Wonderful
Summer Secrets
The Sweetest Thing

<u>The Sanders Brothers Duo</u>
#1 Silent Run
#2 Silent Fall

<u>The Deception Duo</u>
#1 Taken
#2 Played

<u>Angel's Bay Series</u>
Suddenly One Summer
On Shadow Beach
In Shelter Cove
At Hidden Falls
Garden of Secrets
<u>Spin-Off from Angel's Bay</u>
The Way Back Home

About the Author

Barbara Freethy is a #1 New York Times Bestselling Author, a distinction she received for her novel, SUMMER SECRETS. Her 30 novels range from contemporary romance to romantic suspense and women's fiction. Her books have won numerous awards - she is a five-time finalist for the RITA for best contemporary romance from Romance Writers of America and her book DANIEL'S GIFT won the honor and was also optioned for a television movie.

Known for her emotional and compelling stories of love, family, mystery and romance, Barbara enjoys writing about ordinary people caught up in extraordinary adventures. Her latest series, THE WISH SERIES, is being released in 2012. A SECRET WISH, Book #1, was out in January 2012 and JUST A WISH AWAY is being released in May 2012.

Barbara has lived all over the state of California and currently resides in Northern California where she draws much of her inspiration from the beautiful bay area.

Find her on the web at:
www.barbarafreethy.com
www.facebook.com/barbarafreethybooks
www.twitter.com/barbarafreethy

18178517R00121

Made in the USA
Lexington, KY
18 October 2012